MIDNIGHT BLOOD

HARBINGER P.I. BOOK 6

ADAM J WRIGHT

THE HARBINGER P.I. SERIES

DARK PEAK

THE FLAT

THE HAUNTING OF CROW HOUSE
(writing as A.W. James)

It was about nine o'clock in the morning, mid October, with the sun glaring off the wet highway and into my eyes as I drove the Land Rover east out of Dearmont toward the Hawthorne estate.

I'd never heard of the Hawthornes—one of the richest families in Maine—but Felicity had recognized the name straightaway when we'd gotten a call from one of their staff this morning, requesting my presence at the estate at my earliest convenience.

Since we didn't have any ongoing cases at the moment, my earliest convenience was right now. So here I was, driving out to the estate while Felicity stayed in the office in case any more work came in.

The phone wouldn't exactly be ringing off the hook so she was using the spare time to research Arthurian legends, trying to figure out why Sheriff Cantrell had been put into some sort of magical sleep after touching Excalibur in my basement.

As I turned off the highway and followed a long, neat driveway up to a set of wrought-iron gates, I hoped that this job would be simple and would pay well.

We'd put away the Sammy Martin file yesterday, after receiving a letter from his mother that left us in no doubt that the case was closed forever. Both Felicity and I were nursing wounds we'd received while investigating Sammy's disappearance and I wasn't in a hurry to collect any more scars.

A red brick security booth sat by the gate. A guard wearing sunglasses emerged from the door and strode over to the Land Rover. He was dressed in a tight-fitting dark blue uniform and a cap that bore the name *Hawthorne* in white stitched lettering on the front. His bulging biceps and over-developed neck muscles spoke of long hours in the gym. As I wound down the window, he stood with his hands on his hips and shot me a look that was probably unfriendly but was lost behind the shades. "Help you, pal?"

"I'm here to see Charles Hawthorne," I told him. "I'm expected."

"Name?"

"Alec Harbinger."

His steely gaze took in my black jacket, white tee and red flannel shirt and I noticed one eyebrow rise slightly in amusement. I probably wasn't everything the well-dressed preternatural investigator ought to be, at least not in the eyes of this guard or the people who lived in the mansion beyond the gate but he was just going to have to deal with that.

"Yeah, I was told about you." He turned on his heels and went back into the booth. A low buzz sounded from somewhere and the gates swung inward.

I drove forward along a road that curved gently to a gravel parking area in front of the house. There were half a dozen cars sitting there: Ferraris, Bentleys, and Maseratis gleaming in the morning light. I parked the Land Rover some distance away and killed the engine.

As I got out, the house's big double doors opened. A middle-aged man in a butler's uniform came out to greet me. "Mr Harbinger, thank you for arriving promptly. Mr Hawthorne is waiting in the folly."

As I looked at the butler's black morning coat, gray vest, white dress shirt, and black tie, I got the feeling I was underdressed for the impending interview with Mr Hawthorne. As least he wasn't hiring me for my dress sense. I knew as much about Armani as Hawthorne probably knew about killing monsters.

"The folly," I said, trying to remember if I'd been inside a folly ever in my life and deciding quickly that I hadn't. "Lead the way."

He led me to the side of the building where a golf cart waited. I climbed into the passenger side while he got behind the wheel and turned on the engine. The cart purred into life and the butler gently pressed the gas pedal, taking us along a path that cut through a stand of pine trees and then led to a small lake, on the edge of which stood a building that looked like a small Greek temple.

"Does Mr Hawthorne usually conduct business out here?" I asked.

"Not usually, no. But the matter at hand is quite delicate so he would rather speak with you in the folly than in the house."

I turned in my seat to look at the house behind us. Either there was someone in there that Hawthorne didn't want to overhear our conversation or he was embarrassed about hiring a preternatural investigator. This wasn't the first time I'd been hired in a clandestine manner and it probably wouldn't be the last.

The golf cart came to a stop by the faux temple and I got out. Without a word, the butler turned the cart around and drove back toward the house.

I inspected the folly. It had obviously been built by someone with a love of classical Greek architecture, fashioned of white marble with fluted pillars supporting a high, ridged roof. A frieze showed Perseus fighting Medusa, sword raised above his head, ready to strike a blow that would never land because he was nothing more than a piece of sculpted decoration, as was his snake-haired opponent.

"Mr Harbinger." The low voice came from within the structure. I stepped between the pillars, into the folly, where a white marble table sat at the center of a room and similarly carved benches ran along the walls. There was one seat in here that wasn't fashioned of white marble and that was a wheelchair, in which sat a man I guessed to be in his sixties. He wore a tan jacket and trousers and an open-collared, cream-colored shirt. His close-cropped hair and beard were as white as the marble that surrounded us.

"Mr Hawthorne, I presume."

He gave me a curt nod. "You presume correctly. I am Charles Hawthorne. Forgive me for not receiving you at the house but the matter I wish to discuss is rather delicate."

"Understood." As I'd told Felicity recently, everybody hates P.I.s. Even the people who hire us are usually embarrassed about it. "What can I do for you, Mr Hawthorne?"

He pushed a lever on the arm of the wheelchair and it rolled closer to the table. "I need your protection. Someone is trying to kill me with magic."

I indicated one of the stone benches. "May I?"

He nodded. "Of course."

I sat on the hard, smooth surface and said, "Are you sure someone is trying to kill you?"

"Very sure. And don't tell me to go to the police. When you hear what I have to say, you'll see that my situation requires someone in your line of work and not someone who works for the local sheriff's department."

"Okay, I'm listening."

He reached into his jacket pocket and brought out a small leather pouch, which he tossed over to me. I caught it and turned it over in my hands, inspecting it. Symbols were painted in red on the dark leather; a circle, a star, and a cross. I opened the pouch and looked inside. There was some white hair in there and a tiny piece of parchment. I took the parchment out and examined it. More symbols, these written in black ink. A combination of curving lines, geometric shapes, and dots.

"Do you know what those symbols mean?" Hawthorne asked.

"Not exactly but this is a hex bag so they're probably part of some spell or other. I assume the hair in the bag is yours, binding the spell to you. Where did you find this?"

"I discovered it two weeks ago, beneath my bed. I have no idea how long it had been there before that. I only found it because I was looking for my reading glasses, which were missing from the nightstand."

"Were they under the bed too?"

"No, I didn't find them."

"Well, it looks like someone has either hexed you or is trying to scare you." I held the bag up. "Is this why you think someone is trying to kill you?"

"Of course not, do you think I'm a fool? There's more to this than a bag beneath my bed." His gaze moved from me to the quiet lake beyond the pillars. "I used to take great pleasure in walking the grounds of the estate. I'd stroll down to the lake most evenings and sit on the steps of the folly while the sun went down. One evening last week, I sat on the steps over there," he pointed to a set of marble steps that led down to the lake, "and couldn't get up again. All feeling fled from my legs. The doctors have no idea what is wrong with me and I've been confined to this damned wheelchair ever since that day."

"And you think this is connected to the hex bag?"

"The bag," he said, reaching into his pocket, "and this." He placed an object on the marble table. "While I was in the hospital, Wesley, my butler, found this, right here on the table. It must have been there while I was sitting on the steps, just a few feet away, losing the feeling in my legs.

I leaned forward and examined the object. It was a figure made from sticks and white hair that had been twisted and shaped to form a crude likeness of Hawthorne. The legs of the figure had been broken off from the torso and then tied loosely with green string so that they hung uselessly from the figure's body.

"It's voodoo, isn't it?" Hawthorne asked. "A voodoo doll."

"Not necessarily," I told him. "This type of sympathetic magic is practiced in many magical traditions."

"But that's why my legs don't work; because of that...that *thing*."

"We can't say that for sure. It's a possibility, though. Do you have many enemies?"

He scoffed. "I'm a successful businessman, Mr Harbinger. You don't reach the heights I have and not make some enemies. I have rivals, of course. And disgruntled ex-employees. Not to mention colleagues who would like to see me gone."

"But you don't think any of them is doing this," I said. "You think it's someone closer than that. Your staff, perhaps, or even someone in your own family."

He narrowed his eyes. "Why do you say that?"

"Because we're having this conversation in the folly and not in the house. You don't want anyone to overhear us."

Hawthorne seemed to deflate slightly, his body sinking into the wheelchair. A sadness came into his eyes. "I can't rule out anyone in my family as a suspect. There is bad blood between almost all of them. Squabbles, disloyalty, and schemes to outdo each other are commonplace. It's been like that for as long as I can remember. Money and power, Mr Harbinger. They corrupt everyone in the end."

"Then I'm glad I have neither."

He laughed. "I like you. I'm sure you're the right man for this job. And you come highly recommended by Amelia Robinson of Robinson-Lubecki Lumber. I believe you sorted out some trouble for her a few months ago."

The trouble he was referring to was my first case in Dearmont. Amelia Robinson's son had been replaced with a changeling that had tried to steal the family fortune. The creature had killed Amelia's husband in the process. On the way over here, I'd wondered how Charles

Hawthorne had gotten my name and number but now that I knew he was a friend of Amelia Robinson, it made sense.

"You said someone is trying to kill you," I said, picking up the stick figure. "That implies that something else has happened, something more than the loss of your legs. Something that made you finally call me."

"Yes, I was getting to that. Last night, an attempt was made on my life." He spoke calmly, as if he were telling me about the weather. "I was returning home from a meeting in Boston. It was late and my driver, Jonas, was being particularly careful because of the rain. I was tired and decided to take a nap. I had barely closed my eyes when I was woken by Jonas yelling out in surprise. I woke up just as he spun the steering wheel and sent us careening into the woods at the side of the road."

Hawthorne looked shaken for the first time since I'd met him. He stared out at the lake again as if to calm himself and took a deep breath before continuing. "I asked Jonas why he'd done such a damn fool thing and in answer, he pointed back at the road with a trembling hand. There was something standing there, something that wasn't human." He shook his head slightly, as if in disbelief of what he was about to say. "It was a demon. It had wings like a bat and a glowing, hateful stare. I never believed such things existed but I can't dispute what I have seen with my own eyes."

He pointed at the hex bag and the stick figure. "Whoever used those things against me also sent that monster to kill me, I'm certain of it."

"What happened after you drove off the road and saw the creature?" I asked.

"Another car came along the highway and stopped when the driver saw our predicament. He was an off-duty police officer. He made sure Jonas and I were okay and then he called a tow truck."

"And the creature?"

"Gone. The other driver never saw it. I shudder to think what might have happened if he hadn't come along when he did. I'm quite certain Jonas and I would be dead."

I mulled over everything he'd told me. It sounded as if someone was gunning for him and shooting magic bullets. But if someone wanted him dead, why not just use *real* bullets? They tended to be much more reliable than demons.

Sure, summoning a demon to do your dirty work meant that you could be far away from the murder when it happened, and have an airtight alibi, but if the summoner was someone in the Hawthorne family, why were they going to all that trouble? Surely they had enough money to simply hire a hitman and get the same airtight alibi without having to summon a creature from Hell.

"Is anyone in your family interested in the occult?"

He shook his head. "I don't believe so. I'm sure they're all healthily skeptical of such things, as was I until last night."

"Yet you believe one of them could be using magic against you."

"Obviously one of them isn't as skeptical as I thought."

"Tell me about them."

"There's my wife Jane, of course. I'd like to say I trust her implicitly but I can't. That's why she isn't privy to this conversation."

I took a notepad and pencil from my pocket and began taking notes. "Can I ask why you don't trust her?"

"There was... an indiscretion. Jane doesn't know I'm aware of it but I know most things

13

that happen where my family is concerned. You may be the first preternatural investigator in my employ, Mr Harbinger, but I've hired private investigators in the past."

"To follow your wife?"

"Among other things."

"Who did your wife have this indiscretion with? Surely that person is a suspect. They might want you out of the way so the indiscretion can become something more."

He sighed heavily. "No, you're going down the wrong path. My wife and her lover don't seen each other anymore."

I looked up from my notepad. "Are you sure about that?"

"Positive."

I wrote the word *Affair* next to Jane Hawthorne's name and underlined it. I wasn't going to press her husband for the details right now but I'd return to the subject later if I thought it warranted further investigation.

"Does she know about the accident last night?"

"She knows only the lie that I told her: that a drunk driver was heading straight for us and Jonas had to swerve to avoid a head-on collision."

"Okay," I said, "What about your children?"

"Brad is the oldest. He's thirty-two but acts like an eighteen-year-old. Jane and I spoiled him from the moment he was born and now he's only interested in partying and fast cars. He has no sense of responsibility, no ambition."

"Would he be ambitious enough to try and kill you?"

Hawthorne shrugged. "Who knows? At one time, I would have said no but the thought of me being dead could perhaps give him a goal he feels worth pursuing."

"Does he live in the house?"

"Yes. Unlike Elise and Lucy, Brad has never flown the nest."

"Elise and Lucy are your daughters?"

He nodded. "Thankfully, they didn't turn out anything like their brother. Elise is the middle child. She runs a company that promotes businesses on social media. She's good at it, too. Some of her clients are big names in the fashion and food industries. She lives in Portland, where the company is based."

I scribbled all of that into the notepad and then said, "Is there any reason why Elise might want you dead?"

"I don't believe so."

"How about Lucy?"

He stroked his beard for a moment while he considered his answer. When he finally spoke, he said, "Lucy was a strange child. From an early age, she had a fascination with death and dark things. I honestly couldn't say if she's trying to kill me because I don't really know her. I'm not sure anyone does. She's introverted and anti-social, despite her mother's repeated attempts to make her more outgoing."

"Does she live here in the house?"

"No, she moved out a couple of years ago. Said she'd had enough of the arguments and dysfunctional relationships in the family. She lives in Rockport now, in a house paid for by the books she writes." He wrinkled his nose as he said, "Horror fiction. Lucy is the only creative in the family and I have no idea where she inherited it from, certainly not from her mother or from me."

"Do you have any of her books I could take a look at?"

He shrugged. "Brad might have some. I've never read them myself. They're published under a pseudonym. I have no idea what it is. Lucy said she didn't use the family name because she didn't want an advantage when she approached the publisher but I think there's more to it than that. I think she's ashamed of us for some reason."

So he didn't show an interest in his daughter's work. Could that be a motive for her to summon the demon? People have been killed for less but I wasn't going to make any assumptions until I had more evidence.

"It's understandable that she wanted to see if she could make it on her own," I told him.

He scoffed again. "Is it? Why not use every advantage you have? That's the only way to get anywhere in this world."

"Yet Lucy made it without using the Hawthorne name," I said.

"If your idea of 'making it' is locking yourself away from the world and inventing weird stories," he said, "then she's a success. But by normal standards, she's nothing more than a recluse living in a fantasy world."

"Will she speak to me if I need to visit her in the course of my investigation?"

He shrugged. "Possibly. I have no idea."

"Do you have her address?"

"No."

Next to Lucy's name, I wrote *Outcast from*

family. Possible interest in occult. Despite Charles telling me that none of his family members had an interest in the occult, it seemed obvious that Lucy might because of her profession. Maybe Charles didn't consider her a member of the family anymore and had excluded her from his answer to my question because of that.

"As for Brad, Elise, and my wife," Hawthorne said, "You can meet them tonight, at our annual Fall party. Lucy won't deign to make an appearance, of course, but Elise and Brad will be there." He looked at me expectantly, as if I should know what he was talking about.

"Is that a family reunion?" I asked.

He laughed. "You really are new to Dearmont aren't you, Mr Harbinger?"

"Yes, I am," I admitted.

"My wife hosts a party at the house every October. It's a family reunion of sorts, I suppose, but Jane also invites most of the business owners in Dearmont, as well as anyone else of importance. As a Dearmont business owner, you should have received an invitation. I'm surprised you didn't."

"It doesn't surprise me at all," I told him.

"I'm not important; I'm just the local ghost catcher."

"I'll have your name put on the guest list. Then you can come here tonight, meet my family, and tell me which one of them is trying to kill me."

"You think I'll know which of them summoned a demon after a five minute conversation?"

"No, I thought you'd have some sort of tool you could use. A magical item that forces them to tell the truth. Or one that can tell you if they're lying. Since seeing that demon on the road, I've come to the realization that my mind has been closed to many things that could have helped me in the past. Imagine if I had an item such as I just described at a board meeting, or at a meeting with a rival firm. The power I'd have would be unimaginable."

And that's why magic items should be kept away from people like you, I thought to myself.

"I can't force someone to submit to a magical polygraph test," I told him, "Any more than I could force him or her to submit to a mundane one. The use of magic doesn't circumvent ethics. In fact, it makes them even more important."

He frowned, seemingly confused. I should have expected a word like ethics to confuse a man like Charles Hawthorne.

"But if you're not going to use magic, what *are* you going to do?" he asked.

"I'll talk to them, as them some questions."

"I could get any local gumshoe to do that. Tell me why I'm hiring you."

"Because a normal P.I. wouldn't know what they're dealing with. They wouldn't know what questions to ask, what to look for. And most of them wouldn't even believe your story."

He seemed to reflect on that for a moment, his eyes studying the patterns in the marble floor. Then he looked up at me said, "You're right, of course. Very well, come to the party tonight and speak to my family. Report back to me tomorrow and we'll discuss your findings. But if you come up empty-handed, then I expect you to use magic to get results, is that understood?"

"I'll be bringing my associate with me tonight," I said, ignoring the question. "You'll need to put her on the guest list," I said. "Felicity Lake."

"Consider it done."

"I'll take the case, Mr Hawthorne," I said,

"but you need to understand that I work in my own way and in my own time."

He nodded, although there was some reluctance to the movement, and his words were terse when he said, "Just be sure to keep me appraised of your progress."

"I will," I said, putting the hex bag and stick figure into my jacket pocket.

Hawthorne pressed a button on the arm of his wheelchair and said, "Wesley, we're done here. Please take Mr Harbinger back to his car."

"Before I go," I said, turning to a fresh page in my notepad, "Who are the staff working at the house?"

He thought about that for a moment before replying, "The person you're looking for isn't a member of my staff. None of them has any reason to do this to me."

"Still, I'd like to cover all possibilities." I held the pencil over the notepad and looked at Hawthorne expectantly.

He sighed. "Very well. There's Wesley, the butler you've already met. Jonas, my driver who was with me last night. The head chef is named Sofia and she has a staff of three chefs that work for her during various shifts. I don't know their names. And finally, there's our housekeeper Ellen. But as I said, none of these people would want to harm me. We treat our staff very well here."

I wrote the names in the notepad and stood when I heard the golf cart approaching. "I'll see you tonight at the party."

"One more thing, Mr Harbinger," Hawthorne said, looking me over. "It's a formal event, so there is a dress code. You won't need to wear a tuxedo but a suit is a must."

"Not a problem." I said, walking between the pillars and out into the fresh, morning air.

Wesley was turning the golf cart around so that it pointed back along the trail.

As I climbed in, I said, "Have you been working with Charles Hawthorne a long time, Wesley?"

"I've been with Mr Hawthorne all my life," he said proudly. "My father was the butler to the late Edward Hawthorne, Charles's father. Charles and I grew up together."

"So you're friends?"

He looked at me pointedly. "Mr Harbinger, I am not a suspect in this case so I would appreciate it if you didn't interrogate me as if I were."

"Just passing the time," I said, sitting back in the seat.

We passed the rest of the journey in silence. When we got to the house, I jumped out of the cart and Wesley followed me across the gravel to the Land Rover.

"See you tonight," I said, opening the door and getting in behind the wheel.

"Yes, sir." He managed to put enough weight into those two words to tell me he didn't approve of my being here.

I watched him as he went through the double doors and into the house, then I started the engine and backed out of my parking spot, tires crunching on the gravel. When I got to the gate, it swung open. The security guard wasn't anywhere in sight so I assumed he was watching me via the camera that was mounted on his booth.

After driving part of the way through the gate, I stopped and waved at the camera to get his attention. A glass hatch opened and he stuck his head out, his eyes still unreadable behind the shades. "Yeah?" he asked with all the warmth of a block of ice.

"What's your name?"

"What's that got to do with you?"

I shrugged. "It's a simple question. I could drive back there and ask Charles but I don't think he'd appreciate being disturbed again."

He considered that for a moment and then shrugged. "It's Brian."

"Last name?"

"Connors."

I took the notepad out of my jacket pocket, opened it, and added his name to the list of staff members. "Thanks."

"Hey, what are you writing there?"

"Nothing you need to worry about." Throwing the notepad onto the passenger seat, I drove forward and gave him a brief wave as I passed the hatch.

I wasn't sure what to make of the Hawthorne case. It seemed someone was trying to take out Charles Hawthorne by using magic but why not use a more mundane method? Why take away his ability to walk by using an effigy in the folly and not a baseball bat to the knees? Why summon a demon to kill him when hiring an assassin would be so much easier?

It didn't make any sense.

My phone rang. It was Felicity. I pulled over

to the side of the road and answered it. "Hey, what's up?"

"Alec, you need to come back to the office." She sounded concerned.

"What's wrong?"

"I'm not sure exactly. You'd best come back here and see for yourself."

"On my way." I ended the call and put my foot down. As I reached the highway, it began to rain. The wipers came to life and arced back and forth across the windshield in a steady, metronomic rhythm.

I pressed the accelerator and the Land Rover raced along the wet highway.

2

I pushed through the door of my building and ascended the stairs quickly. Felicity met me in the upstairs hallway and gestured to my open office door. The sheriff was in there, sitting in one of the client seats, and so was his daughter Amy.

"I didn't know what else to do," Felicity whispered, "So I told them to wait in there."

"Cantrell's awake," I said, surprised.

"Yes, but there's something strange about him. He looks and sounds like the sheriff but he seems...different in some way." She looked flustered. "Alec, I've got a bad feeling about this. When he looks at me, it's like there's someone else looking out through his eyes."

"Okay, I'll find out why he's here."

"I'll make coffee," Felicity said, quickly disappearing into her office.

I stepped through the office doorway and said, "Hey, guys, what's up?"

When Cantrell turned to face me, I knew what Felicity had meant; he was the same old sheriff but there seemed to be something more behind his eyes than usual, something I couldn't explain.

When no one spoke, I perched on the edge of the desk and said, "Is someone going to tell me what's going on?"

"What's going on," Cantrell said, "is that you were given Excalibur for a reason and you haven't wielded it against your foes yet."

"What?" Now I was confused. This man spoke with the sheriff's voice but he definitely wasn't Cantrell. "Who are you?"

"I am Merlin," he said. "Guardian of the sword given to you by the Lady of the Lake."

There was a crash in the hallway. I turned to see Felicity standing there, staring wide-eyed at Cantrell. The tray of mugs she'd been carrying was on the floor, dark coffee spreading over the linoleum, mixing with milk from the shattered pitcher.

"I'm sorry," Felicity said, crouching down to clean up the mess.

I turned back to the sheriff. "Merlin," I repeated, not sure I'd heard him correctly. "*The* Merlin?"

"There's only one of me, so yes, I am *the* Merlin."

I looked at him closely. "What happened to the sheriff?"

"He is perfectly safe."

"He's stuck in a cave somewhere," Amy said, "While Merlin uses his body." Her eyes were red-ringed, as if she'd been crying. Given the circumstances that were totally understandable.

"That isn't completely true," Merlin said. "Part of John Cantrell is here with me now. I am privy to his memories. He can't share in *my* memories, of course, because he'd go quite mad, so the part of him that is in the cave is resting in an enchanted sleep. It's for the best, believe me."

"Like I said, stuck in a cave," Amy said, "and he won't let my dad out of there until you use Excalibur to defeat a group of evil wizards."

"The Midnight Cabal," Merlin told her. "They killed the Lady of the Forest and that's why Alec was given Excalibur, to avenge her death." He looked at me pointedly. "Not that he's done anything to honor the pledge he made to the Lady of the Lake.

"I don't have any leads yet," I said. But my words didn't sound convincing, not even to me. The truth was, I'd spent two weeks doing nothing after Gloria's death and then the Sammy Martin case had come along and my time had been spent on that.

He narrowed his eyes. "You're stalling, Alec."

"I'm not stalling. And you don't know me, so don't come to my office five minutes after you appear in the modern world and try to psychoanalyze me."

"Alec, listen to him,' Amy said. "You have a job to do. You need to get on that."

"It isn't that simple," I told her. "I know you want your dad back but—"

"It *is* that simple," she said. "Do what you're supposed to do. Then Merlin will release my dad. You help people, don't you? So help my dad. He needs you."

She was right; Sheriff Cantrell was being imprisoned by preternatural means and that situation was squarely in my wheelhouse.

"I'll get on it," I told her.

"Will you, though? Because apparently, you've had this sword for a while and so far, you've done diddlysquat with it. How do I know you're going to do what you say?"

"I said I'll get on it. You'll just have to trust me."

"No, she won't," Merlin said, "because I'll be here to make sure you carry out your duty, Alec."

"Thanks for the offer, but I've got this."

"No," he said, shaking his head, "you haven't 'got this' at all. Did you think the Lady of the Lake would give you such a powerful weapon and then just leave you to your own devices? When Excalibur is wielded on the earthly realm, I act as advisor to its wielder. It isn't an option; I come with the sword. We're a 'package deal,' to use your modern terminology."

I held up my hands in surrender. Something told me that arguing with a legendary wizard from the Middle Ages wasn't going to get me anywhere. Besides, if the legends about him were true, Merlin could be a useful ally in the fight against the Midnight Cabal. I was in no position to refuse his help. I just needed to get used to the fact that he was walking around in the sheriff's body.

"Felicity will do some research into the Cabal," I told him. "If we can track down one of their members or find a lodge, we can probably infiltrate deeper into their organization. I'll contact some people at the Society of Shadows and see if they know of any Cabal locations." My father would be useful right now but since he was missing, I was going to have to rely on his secretary, Michael Chester.

"You see?" Merlin said. "That wasn't so hard, was it? Now we have a plan." He stood and stretched his back, wincing as it cracked audibly. "I'll be back tomorrow. I have some things to attend to."

"Where are you going?" Amy asked him, suddenly panicked. If the fact that Merlin was walking around in Sheriff Cantrell's body was strange to me, it must be doubly so for her. And probably a whole lot scarier.

"I have a job to do," he said. "I'm the sheriff of this town, remember? We can't have the people of Dearmont panicking because I'm not on duty."

She looked confused. "But...you're not the

sheriff. My dad's the sheriff and you're not him."

He spread his arms and looked down at his body and then back at her. "Yes, I am. Don't worry, Amy, I have your father's memories so I know all about police work. I'll do the job just as well as he did it himself." A look of excitement played over his face. "To be honest, I'm looking forward to driving the patrol car."

He directed his gaze at me and his face became stern. "I'll be back tomorrow, Alec, to make sure you're doing the job you swore to do."

As he walked out of the office, Amy got up, pushing her chair back with her legs. "I need to go with him," she told me, "Alec, please do whatever it takes to get my dad back."

"Oh, and Alec," Merlin said, popping his head back through the doorway. "Don't be concerned about working with me. You might think you'd be better off going your own way but believe me, we'll make a great team. I've done this before, you know."

"Yeah," I said, "and look what happened to the last guy."

He looked crestfallen for a moment. "Yes, I see your point. Arthur died in battle." He

seemed to reflect on that for a second and then
became cheery again. "But that won't happen
to you. Arthur's downfall was a quick temper
and a woman who cheated on him. You don't
have either of those, do you?"

"No," I said.

"So everything will be just fine." He smiled
and gave me a thumbs up before leaving.

I wished I could share his optimism but
something inside me kept me cynical. Maybe it
was the fact that every time I teamed up with a
powerful being, something went wrong. In
Paris, I'd worked with Sumiko, a powerful
satori, and come away from that case with some
of my memories wiped. Then Gloria joined my
team for a while and ended up dead. So
working with Merlin, who was probably more
powerful than Sumiko and Gloria combined,
wasn't exactly on my bucket list.

Felicity came into the office with a fresh
tray of coffee. "Where did they go?"

"Merlin's going to play at being a sheriff for
a while."

She set the tray down on my desk. "It's
really him, isn't it? Merlin from the legends."

"Yeah, I think so. He came here to remind
me that I was given Excalibur to avenge

ADAM J WRIGHT

Gloria's death and I should be putting everything else aside to go after the Midnight Cabal."

"He probably doesn't understand that you're running a business."

"He understands, he just doesn't care. As far as he's concerned, we should only be working on the Midnight Cabal case and nothing else." I went to the window and looked out over Main Street. The good folk of Dearmont were going about their business like every other day, unaware that a secret society was plotting their downfall. "I don't know, maybe Merlin is right. I made a pledge to destroy the Cabal and I'm spending my time on other things."

"Like the Hawthorne case?" She joined me at the window, her gaze drawn to the townspeople on the sidewalk. I could smell a tantalizing trace of her perfume, along with something sweet, as if she'd been in her kitchen, baking with sugar and frosting. "How did your meeting with Charles Hawthorne go?"

"He thinks someone—probably a member of his family—is trying to kill him by magical means." I told her everything Hawthorne had told me earlier.

When I finished, Felicity shook her head in

disbelief. "His children," she said softly. "What type of people must they be to do that to their father?"

"If it *is* one of the kids. For all we know, it could be his wife, one of the staff, or even the family dog that wants to kill him." I took the hex bag and stick figure out from my pocket and handed them to her. "Someone used these to attack him."

Felicity held the items at arms length and studied them. "Looks like some sort of sympathetic magic."

"Exactly," I said.

She turned them over in her hands "The fact that these items were used raises a question."

"What's that?"

"Why is someone using magic to harm Charles Hawthorne when they could simply use a gun? Mundane weapons are much more reliable than magical ones."

"I guess that's something we'll discover when we investigate the case. I need you to be my plus-one at a party tonight."

"A party?"

"Yeah, at the Hawthorne house. Everyone in the family is going to be there so it'll give us a chance to question them. Surreptitiously, of course."

Her face lit up. "We're going undercover."

"I guess we are. I mean, we're not using false identities or anything but no one will know why we're really there. Apparently, Jane Hawthorne hosts a party for the business owners in Dearmont every year. Charles put me the guest list."

She frowned in confusion. "If the party is for the owners of Dearmont businesses, shouldn't you be on the list already?"

"I told you, Felicity. Everybody hates P.I.s."

She rolled her eyes. "Maybe the 'P' should stand for paranoid."

"Or maybe it should stand for practical. Anyway, the point is, we're going to the party tonight and it'll give us a chance to suss out the Hawthorne family."

"Do you really think we should be working on this case at all?" she asked, giving the hex bag and stick figure back to me.

"Sure, why not?"

"After what you just said about Merlin and the Midnight Cabal, I thought you were going to focus on that."

"If Charles Hawthorne is right and it's one

of the kids trying to murder him, we'll be able to crack the case in one evening. I'll take a crystal shard to the party and that will let us know who's been using magic recently. We get free food and drink and collect a big paycheck when we solve the case. And then we'll be free to work on the Cabal stuff tomorrow. I'm not seeing a downside."

"Well, if you think it's going to be that easy," she said uncertainly.

"I do. All we have to do to make sure there are no loose ends is drive to Rockport today and pay a visit to the one member of the Hawthorne family who won't be at the party tonight."

"Lucy Hawthorne. The reclusive author."

I nodded. "I'm pretty sure there's no love lost between Charles and Lucy so she'd be a good place for us to start. And Rockport is only forty-minutes from here."

"But if she's a recluse, will she even speak to us?"

I walked over to my desk and took a crystal shard from the drawer. "We just need to get close enough to use this," I said, holding it up. It was glowing because of its close proximity to the hex bag and figure. "If it glows when we get

ADAM J WRIGHT

near Lucy, we know she's been using magic and she becomes our number one suspect. If it doesn't, we drive back to Dearmont and never bother her again."

She offered me a thin smile. "You make it sound so simple."

I shrugged. "It sounds simple because it *is* simple."

"I'll get my things," she said, leaving the office.

I slipped the crystal shard into my pocket and threw the hex bag and stick figure into the desk drawer.

When I left the room, Felicity was waiting in the hall outside, her laptop under her arm.

"You going to do some research on the way?" I asked.

"Well I assume we'll need her address. Unless Charles gave it to you."

I shook my head and began descending the steps to the door. "No, he didn't know it."

"So we'll need the laptop," she said, following me outside.

3

As we drove south out of Dearmont, the sun was high in the sky, illuminating the edges of dark storm clouds that promised rain but hadn't delivered on that promise yet.

I had the radio on low, tuned to a Bangor rock n' roll station. Dire Straits were singing *Money For Nothing* and I was humming along, low enough that I didn't disturb Felicity.

She was tapping away at the laptop's keyboard, the screen's bluish glow reflecting in her glasses. Behind that reflected glow, her dark eyes were narrow with concentration.

"You got anything?" I asked her.

She looked up from the screen and glanced at me as if in a daze. She'd been so focused on her research that it probably wouldn't have mattered if I'd had the radio cranked up full blast. "Hmm? Oh, yes, I found her address ten minutes ago. I'm looking at the books she writes."

"You found her pen name?"

Felicity nodded. "She writes under the name L.H. Cane. I assume the L.H. stands for Lucy Hawthorne. Her books seem to be horror with an occult flavor. It sounds like there are some Lovecraftian themes in her writing and she lists Lovecraft as one of her influences, as well as Algernon Blackwood, Arthur Machen, Thomas Tryon, and Stephen King."

"So we know she at least has a passing interest in the occult," I said.

"But that doesn't mean she tried to murder her father."

"No, it doesn't," I agreed. "How many books has she written? What are the titles?"

"There are quite a few. *The Witch Moon, The House by the Sea*, a book of short stories called *Crawling From the Darkness. The Dream Portal, The Face of the Monster*. There are dozens of them. Shall I go on?"

"Anything about demons?"

She scanned down the list, using her fingernail as a guide. "There's one here called

The Summon. I suppose that could be about demons. And there's one called *Beasts From Hell*."

"When she researched those books, maybe she discovered a way to summon demons."

Felicity shrugged. "It's possible, I suppose."

"You don't sound convinced."

"It's just that she seems like the type of person who wants to distance herself from her family. Why would she break her period of isolation from them to attack her father?"

"Revenge, maybe. We don't know what happened in the past. It could have taken this long for her desire for revenge to boil over and prompt her to take action."

Felicity went back to looking at the laptop, seemingly unconvinced by my theory.

The storm clouds finally delivered on their promise and broke open. I turned on the wipers and concentrated on the road ahead as heavy rain lashed at the windshield and bounced off the Land Rover's hood. Dire Straits finished singing about money for nothing and November Rain by Guns n' Roses started to come through the speakers. The timing of the song and the sudden precipitation was eerie.

Forty-five minutes later, we reached Rockport. As we drove into town, Felicity gave me directions that took us past the harbor and then along a street that was lined with long, well-manicured lawns and federal style houses. The houses were situated some distance away from each other and tall pine trees bordered each property, offering privacy. We got all the way to the end of the street when Felicity pointed at a house on the right and said, "That one."

I pulled over and killed the engine. Lucy Hawthorne's house was identical to the others; a large three-story federal style building set back from the sidewalk behind a long, neat lawn. The driveway was empty. If Lucy was at home, her car was probably sitting in the closed garage that sat beside the house.

Felicity inspected the building through her window. "What a lovely place. I bet she has a view of the harbor through the rear windows."

"You want to go knock on the door?" I asked her. "She might be more likely to open it if there's only one person standing there."

"All right. Give me the crystal shard."

I handed it to her and she opened her door. The smell of wet leaves and grass entered the car, along with the hissing of the rain. "Wish me luck."

"Good luck."

She flicked the hood of her jacket over her head and climbed out of the Land Rover, holding the hood to her head as she ran up the driveway toward the house. I wondered if she was going to tell Lucy some story explaining her presence or if she'd simply hold the crystal shard close to the girl and then run back down the driveway. Knowing Felicity, I had a hard time picturing the second scenario. She'd be more likely to talk to Lucy, get to know her.

Of course, if Lucy didn't answer the door at all, then we were going to have to come up with another plan.

Through the rain-smeared window, I watched Felicity ascend a small flight of steps to the front porch and lift the knocker on the tall front door three times. Protected from rain by the covered porch, she pushed the hood down off her head.

"Come on," I whispered, willing Lucy Hawthorne to open the door.

A couple of long minutes passed and nothing happened. Felicity raised and lowered the knocker again. This time, I was sure I saw a curtain twitch behind one of the first floor windows.

Felicity turned toward me and shrugged. Then she turned back to the front door quickly, as if she'd heard movement in the house. But the door remained closed.

After another minute or so, Felicity came back to the car. "No answer," she said as she climbed into the Land Rover, bringing the rain and a rotten-leaf scented breeze with her. "I think she's in there, though. I'm sure I heard someone inside the house."

I shrugged. "Well, her father said she was reclusive so I guess expecting her to answer the door was a long shot. Let's go and grab a burger at Darla's."

"Sounds good."

I started the engine and turned up the heater for Felicity.

When I reached the intersection at the end of the street, I glanced at Lucy's house in the rearview mirror. In the first floor window where I'd seen the curtains twitch earlier, a face peered out at us.

4

Darla's Diner was busy, as usual, but Felicity and I managed to get a booth by the window. After we'd ordered, I watched the rain falling over the parking lot while Felicity tapped away on her laptop.

"Do you still think this case is going to be solved by the morning?" she asked, peering at me over the top of her glasses.

I shrugged. "Sure, why not?"

"Well, we didn't manage to eliminate Lucy Hawthorne as a suspect and all we had to do was get her to answer the door. Do you think the other family members will be any easier?"

"They'll be at the party. We'll have easy access to them," I said. "Whoever makes the crystal glow, that's our culprit."

"And if none of them has any magical residue?"

"Then we move our attention back onto Lucy."

She looked out of the window at the rain and the cars.

"You okay?" I asked her.

"Hmm? What do you mean?"

"You seem to be pondering something."

She hesitated, as if determining how to frame her next sentence, and then said, "You haven't mentioned the Midnight Cabal all day."

"What's that supposed to mean?"

"Merlin won't release the sheriff until you use Excalibur to attack the Cabal and yet here we are spending our time chasing down the children of a billionaire."

"Charles Hawthorne's life might be at stake."

"So might Sheriff Cantrell's. I can't bear to think of him trapped in some magical prison while Merlin is walking around in his body." She leaned forward and lowered her voice. "And if the person attacking Hawthorne wanted to kill him, they'd simply have broken the neck on that effigy, not just its legs. I think someone wants Charles Hawthorne to suffer but they don't necessarily want him dead."

"Well I'm sure the truth will come out during our investigation."

She sat back in her seat and looked like she was about to say something but stopped herself when the waitress arrived at our table with the food. We sat in silence as the burgers and sodas were placed in front of us and Felicity gave the waitress a warm smile. But after the waitress had left, Felicity's demeanor became frosty. She leaned toward me. "I don't think you should be investigating the Hawthorne case."

That was a surprise. She'd seemed onboard with the investigation until now. "What's your problem?" I asked.

She took a deep breath, as if steeling herself, and then said, "The problem isn't mine, Alec. The problem is yours. You're avoiding the Cabal because your mother is a member of the organization. And you're using the Hawthorne case as a distraction."

"Wow," I said, stunned. "I'm pretty sure we discussed this before and I said I'd take down the Cabal no matter who its members were."

"You did," she conceded. "But since then you haven't done anything about it. At first, that was totally understandable; I could see why you'd put it off. But now, the longer you procrastinate, the longer the sheriff is trapped in some magical prison. Amy has to deal with Merlin inhabiting her father's body. And what will happen to Dearmont now that there's an ancient wizard pretending to be the sheriff?"

"I'm sure Amy won't let anything bad happen to the town," I said.

"That's not the point. She needs her father back. We need our sheriff back. You're supposed to help people in danger from preternatural beings and Sheriff Cantrell is the very definition of that at the moment."

"Charles Hawthorne is also in danger," I reminded her.

"So give me the Hawthorne case."

"What?"

"Give me the case. I'll find out who's trying to hurt Hawthorne, freeing up your time so you can work with Merlin to bring down the Cabal."

I took a bite of my burger and thought about that for a moment. I had no doubt that Felicity could handle the Hawthorne case— hell, I had no doubt that she could handle *any* case—but giving this case to her at this moment meant that I would have to focus all my attention on the Midnight Cabal.

And I knew deep down that Felicity was right; I'd been avoiding the Cabal because of my mother's ties to it.

After Gloria's death, I'd been filled with rage and I'd sworn to take down the Cabal no matter what. The fact that my mother was a senior member in the organization hadn't mattered to me; if she was one of the Cabal, then she had to go down, just like every other member.

At least, that was what I'd told myself at the time. But as the weeks wore on, I realized that I had no idea what had really happened on the night my mother had disappeared, the night I'd thought she'd been killed.

For twenty years, she'd been alive and hadn't contacted me. Not only that, she'd been working with my enemies. Why? What had happened to make her go over to the Cabal?

I needed answers more than I needed revenge. But because I'd pledged vengeance to the Lady of the Lake and had received Excalibur from her, I was on a path of bloodshed. And Merlin was going to make sure I stayed on that path until I destroyed every member of the Midnight Cabal, including my mother.

"Okay," I told Felicity. "I'll give you the Hawthorne case. If we can't solve it tonight at the party, it's all yours. I'll work with Merlin and do the Cabal thing."

She nodded slowly and looked at me with compassion in her dark eyes. "You're worried about your mother, aren't you? Wondering where she fits into all of this?"

"Yeah," I admitted. "For most of my life, I thought she was dead. Then I discover that not only is she alive, she's part of an enemy organization. It's crazy."

"I'm sure everything will work out," Felicity said, her tone lacking conviction.

"Will it? What if Merlin and I crash a Cabal party and he starts throwing magic missiles around the place? He might kill my mother before I get a chance to speak with her. I'll never know what happened to her that night after she told me to run from the car. I won't know why she let me think she was dead for all these years, why she joined the Cabal. It'd be like losing her all over again."

Felicity reached across the table and placed

her hand on mine. "Don't worry, Alec, I'm sure you'll get your answers."

I shrugged, unable to share her optimism. "Yeah, maybe."

"I think Merlin's being unrealistic if he expects you to bring down the entire Cabal anyway."

"Yeah, the Society has been fighting the Cabal for centuries and hasn't managed to destroy it completely. I don't know why Merlin thinks I have a chance of succeeding where an entire secret society failed."

"The Society doesn't have Excalibur," she said.

"Do you think the sword is that powerful?"

"King Arthur built an entire kingdom with the help of that sword."

"I don't want to build a kingdom; I just want to kill a few bad guys."

"Then there shouldn't be any problem." She smiled, let go of my hand, and took a bite of her burger.

We ate in silence, comfortable enough in each other's company that we didn't feel the need to make small talk. I watched the rivulets of rain running down the window and wondered how I was going to get a lead on the

Midnight Cabal. Merlin wanted some solid intel by tomorrow morning.

My best course of action would probably be to make a call to the Society and see if they had any leads. I could speak to my father's secretary, and see if he knew anything about Cabal activity in this area. The closer to Dearmont the better. There was no way I was going on a road trip with Merlin.

"That was lovely," Felicity said after she'd finished her burger.

"Yeah," I said through a mouthful of fries. "The food's always great here. You want anything else?"

She nodded. "I'm going to have a piece of strawberry cheesecake. How about you?"

"No," I said, pushing my empty plate away. "If I eat another bite, I won't fit into my suit tonight."

"Your loss," she said before catching the waitress's attention and ordering the cheesecake.

After we finished lunch and we were back in the Land Rover with the heavy rain pattering against the windshield and blurring the outside world, I told Felicity about my plan to call the Society of Shadows and press them for info on recent Midnight Cabal activity.

She checked her watch and said, "You might as well do that now. It will be late evening in London."

I could see she wasn't going to stop pushing until I'd taken some action regarding the Cabal so I grabbed my phone and called the number that was listed in my contacts as Mysterium Import and Export, the cover name for the Society of Shadow's headquarters in London, England.

A female voice answered and I asked for Michael Chester. I didn't need to tell her who I was because the Society's phone operators had access to a magical ID check that went way beyond simple voice recognition.

When Michael answered, he sounded weary. "Alec, what can I do for you? If you're calling about your father, we still don't know his whereabouts."

"Actually, I'm calling about the Midnight Cabal. I want to know if they've been active anywhere around here. You have any info that could lead me to a local lodge?"

"You having a slow day?" he asked me. "P.I.s

don't usually go in search of the Cabal. You guys usually leave that to the Shadow Watch."

The Shadow Watch was an organization within the Society that acted as an army and intelligence service rolled into one.

Now that the Society knew the Midnight Cabal—which it had thought defunct since the 18th Century—still existed, the Watch was tasked with seeking out and destroying Cabal strongholds. Some of its members worked as undercover agents while others were part of an army that used magic as well as conventional weapons to fight the enemy.

"Yeah, well, humor me," I said to Michael. "If I wanted a lead on the Cabal, where would be a good place to start?"

There was a short silence on the other end of the line and then he sighed and said, "You're in Dearmont, Maine, right?"

"That's right."

"I'll see what I can dig up. I have a couple of contacts in the Watch. Maybe I can get you the name of a Cabal member or something."

"That's great."

"I'm not promising anything," he said. "Those guys are secretive at the best of times."

"You know where to reach me," I told him and hung up.

Turning to Felicity, I said, "He's going to look into it."

"Good. Hopefully we can get the sheriff back fairly soon."

I didn't say anything. Felicity's optimism wasn't something I shared. Finding the Cabal was one thing, destroying it was something else entirely.

Starting the car, I said, "It'll probably take a while for Michael to get back to me. In the meantime, we have a party to attend."

5

When we arrived at the Hawthorne house, the gravel parking area was full of vehicles. A parking attendant used an illuminated orange baton to wave me into a parking space between a Volvo sedan and a Ford Taurus.

As I got out of the Land Rover, the crisp, night air chilled me through my suit. I hadn't worn it in a while and it felt a little tight on the biceps, shoulders, and chest but it would have to do.

Felicity looked amazing in an off the shoulder black Bardot dress. I had no idea what the dress was called until she told me on the way over here that the neckline was named after the actress Brigitte Bardot.

Felicity's dark hair was pinned up on top of

her head and she'd eschewed her glasses in favor of contact lenses. A silver chain adorned her left wrist and in that hand, she carried a black clutch purse that contained, among other things, a magical crystal shard. I also had a crystal shard. Mine was in my pocket.

"Let's get inside," I said. "It's freezing out here."

We followed a number of other smartly dressed people through the open front doors and into a grand foyer where waiters and waitresses were walking around with silver trays of hors d'oeuvres and drinks. Felicity accepted a glass of white wine but refused an appetizer.

I took the proffered wine and a piece of rye bread topped with smoked salmon. As we followed the flow of guests from the foyer into a high-ceilinged room where a string quartet was set up in the corner and a number of guests were mingling and chatting, I took a bite of the hors d'oeuvre and nodded in appreciation.

"Hey, this is good," I told Felicity. "You should try one."

"Perhaps I will later but for now, I'm trying to concentrate on the job at hand." Her eyes scanned the room and I assumed she was hunting for members of the Hawthorne family.

"Me too," I said. "But if I see deviled eggs, I won't be held responsible for my actions."

"I can't see any of the Hawthornes," Felicity said, ignoring me. "It's very crowded."

She was right. The room was huge by anyone's standards but the guests filled it easily. As well as the music provided by the string quartet, a low hum of constant chatter filled the air, along with the mingled scents of various perfumes and colognes and a faint smell of tobacco. Far from being pleasant, the atmosphere was claustrophobic.

"There must be hundreds of people here," I said. "I guess everyone wants to be seen at Jane Hawthorne's gathering. What do you think they use this room for when they're not having a party?"

"It's a ballroom," Felicity said. "Its only purpose is to hold gatherings like this. It's probably the largest room in the house yet despite its size, there's a huge gold-framed mirror on the wall to make the space look even more vast. It's all very ostentatious."

I looked at the mirror she was referring to. It covered almost one entire wall, its gold frame adorned with fine filigree and carvings of cherubim. The reflection of the room in which we stood caused an optical illusion that made it look as if the ballroom were twice its actual size.

"Hey, Alec!"

I turned to see Leon navigating his way through the crowd, holding a red-colored cocktail aloft as he maneuvered around the people in his path. When he reached me, he shook my hand and said, "Long time no see, man." Then he turned to Felicity and gave her a brief hug. "Felicity, you look amazing."

"Thank you, Leon," she said, smiling. "I didn't know you'd be here."

"Yeah, I get an invitation every year because I know Brad Hawthorne a little. The fact that I'm rich may have something to do with it too. Actually, I probably only get invited because I'm rich."

"How well do you know Brad?" I asked.

Leon shrugged. "We've crossed paths a few times at various parties but we're not buddies or anything."

"Is he here tonight?" Felicity asked. "We can't see him."

"Yeah, he's around here somewhere. I saw

him earlier." He scanned the crowd and then shook his head. "I don't see him right now though."

"What about the other members of the family?" I asked. "Do you know them too?"

"Yeah, a little."

"What can you tell me about them?"

Leon looked at me closely and narrowed his eyes. "I knew this wasn't your scene." He lowered his voice. "You're here on a case aren't you?"

I said nothing.

"Tell me what's going on, man. Maybe I can help."

"Nothing's going on," I told him. "We just want to talk to the Hawthorne family." I didn't see any reason to tell Leon what Felicity and I were up to because as far as I was concerned, this case would be closed by the time this party was over.

Yeah, I really thought it was going to be that simple.

"They're all here somewhere," he said. "Jane usually wanders around the room making sure the guests are happy but I don't see her at the moment. Charles is less friendly than his wife and normally stands by the fireplace over there scowling and nursing a drink. I guess he won't be doing that this year, though, because I heard he's in a wheelchair now."

"There he is," Felicity said, pointing through the crowd at Charles Hawthorne. He'd entered through a door at the far end of the room and was cutting a path through the crowd with his wheelchair. A shot glass of whisky on the arm of the chair was so full that the liquid spilled over the rim of the glass. Charles's face was set into a scowl, which he seemed to have adopted to let everyone around him know that he didn't want company.

"Leon! Dude!"

I turned to see a tall fair-haired young man slap his arm around Leon's shoulder.

Leon grinned but the gesture seemed forced. "Hey, Brad, how's it going?"

Brad rolled his eyes. "You know how it is, dude. Things are pretty lame at the moment. Everything's so boring. Not to mention I have to wear this stupid suit to this stupid party." His face suddenly brightened as if he'd had the best idea in the world. "Hey, you wanna come up to my room and play some games? I've got some new ones."

"No can do, man," Leon said. "Maybe some other time, okay?"

I slipped the crystal shard out of my jacket pocket and held it in a loose fist, surreptitiously moving it closer to Brad. The crystal didn't glow at all. Actually, I'd have been surprised if it had; Brad was way down on my suspect list.

"These are my friends," Leon told Brad. "Alec Harbinger and Felicity Lake."

Brad shook our hands and said, "Hey, good to meet you." He pointed at me and frowned. "Don't I know you from somewhere?"

"I don't think so," I said.

"You were on TV weren't you? When that kid went missing?"

"Yeah, that was me."

"You're a P.I. right?"

I nodded.

"They ever find that kid?"

I shook my head. Felicity and I knew exactly where Sammy Martin was but we weren't telling.

"If you ever need any work, ask my dad," Brad said. "He hires private eyes all the time."

"I'm not a private eye," I told him. "I'm a preternatural investigator."

He looked at me as if I'd just grown two heads. "Oh, you're one of those guys. Ghosts and goblins, right? This must be the busiest time of the year for you with Halloween coming soon."

I gave him a flat smile and said nothing.

"Anyhoo, I'm going to go find some more alcohol," he said. "There's only so much socializing I can handle while sober. My sister had the right idea when she put this family in her rearview, know what I mean?"

"Have you seen Lucy lately?" I asked him. Unlike Brad, she was at the top of my list of suspects. That was why I'd thought it worth driving to Rockport earlier. If any of the Hawthorne children were involved in witchcraft, Lucy seemed the most likely candidate.

Brad thought for a moment and then shook his head. "Not for a while, man. She sends me her books every time a new one comes out because she knows I'm a fan but I haven't seen her in person for..." He frowned while he thought about it and then said, "...over a year. Wow, I didn't realize it was that long. I should call her sometime."

"What about your dad?" I asked him. "Does he have any contact with Lucy?"

He let out a short laugh. "Ha, no way. Dad thinks she's weird, which she kinda is, I guess. I'm fine with it but Dad doesn't do weird. He and Lucy were always fighting because she wouldn't fall into line. She did her own thing and Dad didn't like that. He has a stick up his ass most of the time."

"Brad, you shouldn't speak about your father that way!" An elegant blonde lady stepped into our little group. She wore a black dress that hugged her figure all the way down to her ankles. I could see the resemblance between her and Brad and knew at once that this was the hostess of the evening.

"Jane Hawthorne," she said, reaching for my hand. Her touch was warm and light. "Please ignore my son; he likes to stir up drama where none exists. And you are?"

"Alec Harbinger," I said. "And this is my associate Felicity Lake."

"So glad you could make it," Jane said, either not recalling or choosing not to mention the fact that she hadn't invited us here. As she shook Felicity's hand, she said, "You look wonderful, Miss Lake. You must tell me where you got that delightful chain."

"I'm out of here," Brad said, rolling his eyes. "Later, dudes." He disappeared into the throng of people.

Turning back to me, Jane asked, "What is it you do, Mr Harbinger?"

"I'm a preternatural investigator," I told her, choosing to avoid confusion by using the full words of my job title rather than the initials.

"Oh," she said uncertainly. "That sounds very…interesting."

While Jane's attention was focused on me, Felicity opened her purse and took out a crystal shard. There was no glow.

"Well, enjoy the party," Jane said, seeming a little flustered at my profession. Or maybe she'd suddenly remembered that she hadn't sent me an invitation and was wondering how I'd gotten in here. She gave me an uncertain wave and disappeared into the crowd.

"Okay," Leon said, after Jane had gone. "You have to tell me what's going on here. I saw those crystal shards. Why are you checking people for residual magic?"

"We're working a case," I conceded. "But at the moment, all we're doing is eliminating people from our investigation. There's nothing major happening, it's just routine."

Leon looked unconvinced but I wasn't going to lay the entire case out for him right now. Maybe once we'd found our culprit I'd explain everything to him but for now, I couldn't risk being overheard by the very people we were investigating.

I saw a flash of red hair and my heart sank when I recognized Amy. Not because Amy was here at the party but because Merlin—in the shape of her father, of course—was accompanying her.

Felicity looked over and saw them too. "Well you should have guessed the sheriff would be invited to Jane Hawthorne's party, Alec."

"Yes, of course," I said, "But what's he doing here? He *isn't* the sheriff so why is he here at all?"

She shrugged. "If you were trapped in a cave for hundreds of years, wouldn't you want to go to a party when you got out?"

I let out a long sigh. Coming here was beginning to look like a mistake. The last thing I needed was another lecture from Merlin about how I should be doing my duty. Amy would take the opportunity to twist the knife by telling me how desperately her father needed me.

I had nothing new to offer in the way of leads or information because I was still waiting to hear from Michael Chester so the conversation would be a repeat of the one we'd had earlier in my office, with me feeling like the bad guy.

"Come on, guys," Leon said. "I can see this is more than just routine. Tell me what's—"

He stopped suddenly and I turned to look at him. He was staring at something across the room.

I followed his gaze to the huge mirror on the wall. The edges of the glass were darkening, as dark smoke spread across the reflection of the room in which we stood. The smoke expanded until it obscured the glass entirely and the mirror became a huge square of impenetrable darkness on the wall.

The chatter in the room had died down. Everyone's attention seemed fixed on the mirror. Some of the guests were cooing appreciatively, as if this sudden apparition was part of the evening's entertainment.

I took the crystal shard out of my pocket. It was glowing as brightly as a tiny sun.

The dark smoke erupted from the mirror and filled the ballroom in a matter of seconds. No one was cooing now.

The thick smoke brought a fetid stench of sulfur with it and most of the guests were now either coughing or gagging. Everyone began running and stumbling for the door.

Felicity looked at me with concern in her eyes. "Alec, what's happening?"

"I have no idea." Standing here doing nothing wasn't an option; this could be another magical attack on Charles. I looked for him in the chaos but the smoke was so thick that visibility was reduced to no more than a few feet.

"Follow me," I said to Felicity and Leon.

Instead of heading for the door, which would be blocked by panicked guests trying to escape the room, I made my way to the window and opened it before climbing out onto a strip of grass near the parking area.

While Felicity and Leon clambered out of the window, I sprinted to the Land Rover and opened the tailgate.

The scene out here was no less chaotic than

inside. Guests were stampeding out of the mansion, most of them running for their cars. Some of them were chatting hurriedly into their phones as they called the police and fire departments.

I opened the false bottom of the Land Rover's trunk and unrolled a length of burlap, revealing the four enchanted swords and four daggers within. Felicity arrived next to me and I handed one to her. Its blade took on a blue glow as she wrapped her fingers around the grip.

I gave another sword to Leon and as he took it in his hand, its blade glowed likewise.

Taking a sword for myself and closing the tailgate, I said, "Come on, let's see what we're dealing with here. Our first objective is to make sure everyone gets out of the building safely."

We ran back to the window and climbed inside. The ballroom was still full of the foul-smelling smoke but it drew back from the glow of our swords. "Put the blades together," I said.

I held my blade out in front of me. Leon, on my right, and Felicity, on my left, did the same, touching the tips of their blades to mine. This formed a wedge of blue light ahead of us from which the black smoke recoiled.

"Anyone who is still in the room, follow the light," I shouted. Then, to Felicity and Leon, I said, "We're going to make our way to the door."

I heard people around me as we made our way to the door. They followed the light of our swords and blurted out questions.

"What happened?"

"Is the house on fire?"

"Are we under attack?"

I had no answers for them. I simply led them to the ballroom door so they could join the other guests leaving the mansion via the foyer.

Someone grabbed my shoulder and I turned to see it was Jane Hawthorne. "Have you seen Charles?" she asked. Brad and a girl I assumed to be Elise stood next to her. Brad's laid-back attitude was gone, replaced by something approximating terror.

"Don't worry," I told them. "We're going back in there. We'll find him."

She nodded uncertainly, her eyes drawn to the three glowing swords. "Okay. I'll make sure everyone here gets out safely." She turned away from us and raised her voice as she spoke to the guests. "Please leave in an orderly manner. There's nothing to worry about. Just make your way outside and we'll let the fire department handle this."

I was pretty sure this smoke was beyond the fire department's bailiwick. The way it had come out of the mirror like that meant it was magical in nature, probably summoned here for some purpose. Since we were here because Charles Hawthorne thought someone was trying to kill him with magic, that purpose seemed all too obvious.

"We have to find Charles Hawthorne," I said to Leon and Felicity. "He's still in there somewhere."

We formed a wedge of light again and re-entered the thick smoke. I called Charles's name but there was no answer.

I could hear footsteps on the ballroom floor; there were still other guests in here, lost in the smoke.

"Open all the windows," I told Felicity and Leon.

We split up and opened the windows in an attempt to disperse the smoke. The cold of the night entered the ballroom, chilling the air. I rejoined my friends and we called Charles's name again.

This time, I got an answer but it wasn't Charles who answered my call, it was Amy. "He's over here."

I followed the sound of her voice, quickening my pace as I made out figures through the dispersing smoke. When I reached Amy, I found her crouched down next to Charles Hawthorne's prone body. The wheelchair was on its side, the shot glass smashed. Whisky covered the floor.

"Charles!" I said, crouching down and feeling for a pulse.

"He's alive," Amy said. "He's just blind drunk. Someone probably knocked him over in their haste to get out of here."

Merlin was standing nearby, looking at the smoke around us with interest. He made a complicated gesture with his hands and nodded to himself, seemingly satisfied with something.

"What was that?" I asked him. "What did you just do?"

"I merely ascertained the nature of the magic that fills this room."

Leon, who had no idea Sheriff Cantrell was

being possessed by Merlin, raised an eyebrow and said, "What the hell?"

"And what is the nature of the magic?" I asked Merlin.

He grabbed a handful of the smoke and wafted it in my direction. "This is a smoke of illusion. It gives the intended recipient frightful visions. I've used it myself on the battlefield on a couple of occasions. It can send an entire army of enemy soldiers fleeing for their lives, even though the phantoms they see are merely creations of their own minds."

"I didn't see any phantoms in the smoke," I told him. "Did anyone else?"

Leon and Felicity shook their heads.

"This spell was intended for one recipient only," Merlin said. He pointed at the prone body of Charles Hawthorne.

"And it knocked him out?" I asked.

He shook his head. "The whisky did that. Mr Hawthorne was already drinking himself into oblivion before the smoke manifested."

Charles rolled onto his side and groaned. He didn't look like the fall from the chair had hurt him. There weren't any bruises or cuts that I could see.

Leon and I grabbed him under his armpits

and lifted him into the wheelchair. Charles lolled to one side and opened his bleary eyes. "I had a terrible dream. It was in the smoke." He lifted a finger to point at the thinning smoke and then dropped his arm as if it were heavy as lead.

"What was it?" I asked. "What did you see?" Maybe the nature of the illusion would reveal who sent it.

"The car wreck. Oh God, it was horrible. I don't want to see that again. I don't want to think about it." His bloodshot eyes searched for something. When they didn't find it, Charles said, "Whisky. Where's my whisky?"

"Oh my god, Charles, you're all right!"

Jane was running across the ballroom toward us with a look of relief on her face.

He saw her and let out a long, deep sigh. "Get me out of here, Harbinger. I don't want to talk to that woman."

"Not my problem," I said. "My job is to find out who cast that spell, not help you deal with your marital difficulties."

Jane reached him and threw her arms around him. Charles scowled at me.

In the distance, I could hear sirens cutting through the night. Turning to Merlin, I said,

"That's the police and the fire department. You should probably deal with them, Sheriff."

Before he had a chance to answer, I headed for the door with Felicity and Leon. I was pissed because someone had managed to attack Charles right under my nose and this case was obviously not going to be as simple as I'd first thought.

In the foyer, I saw Brad talking to the girl I'd earlier assumed to be his sister. To make sure, I went up to her and said, "Excuse me, are you Elise Hawthorne?"

She turned to me and nodded. "Yes. Yes, I am."

I took the crystal shard out of my pocket and held it up to her. There was no glow.

"Thanks." I left the foyer and went outside, leaving a confused Elise Hawthorne in my wake.

When I got to the Land Rover, I replaced the swords in their burlap wrapping and stowed them.

The police cars were arriving at the gate now, their flashing lights illuminating the faces of the guests standing in the parking area. Merlin and Amy were walking across the gravel to meet them. I wasn't sure what Merlin was going to tell them but I was sure he'd think of something.

Leon grabbed my arm and said, "You have to tell me what the hell is happening. Because that guy looks like the sheriff but he isn't the sheriff."

"I'll explain everything," I said. "But not here. Meet me at Darla's." I wasn't going to stand here chatting about the Hawthornes but I owed Leon an explanation. He'd been with me on some of my toughest cases and had picked up a sword tonight without hesitation, even though he had no idea what we might be facing.

"Cool, see you there." He went to his car, or maybe I should say *tonight's* car, since Leon owned a fleet of them and changed them regularly. Tonight, he was driving a white Ferrari Testarossa that looked like it came straight out of an episode of Miami Vice.

I climbed into the Land Rover, expecting Felicity to get into the passenger seat, but she remained outside. Winding down the window, I said, "You coming?"

"Just give me a minute. There's something I have to do." She turned away and walked toward the gate, waving to Leon as he purred past her in his Ferrari on the way to Darla's. I watched as Felicity approached Amy and spoke to her for a couple of minutes before returning to the Land Rover and getting in beside me.

"What was that about?"

"I invited Amy to join us at Darla's."

"What? Why?"

"This is my case now, remember? I want Amy to help me solve it. She wants her dad back as soon as possible and she's going to want to help in some way. So she can work with me on the Hawthorne case."

"Okay."

"I'll probably get the Blackwell sisters to help as well."

"So you get the entire Scooby Gang while I'm stuck with that old wizard?"

She smiled and shrugged. "Maybe next time you'll think twice before swearing an oath to a faerie in a pond."

"Yeah," I said, starting the engine. "Maybe I will."

6

Leon sat back in his seat and shook his head as if in disbelief of what we'd just told him. He looked from Amy to Felicity and then to me. "Merlin? That's wild, man!"

"It's very worrying," Amy told him.

His face became serious. "Yeah, of course. I'll help in any way I can."

I picked up the last chicken finger from my plate—we'd ordered a number of dishes and shared them while we'd talked to Leon—and said, "We want you to work on the Hawthorne case with Felicity and Amy while I track down the Midnight Cabal with Merlin."

He nodded enthusiastically. "Count me in."

"That's settled then," I said. I was less than happy with the arrangement. Going after the

Midnight Cabal meant that at some point in the future I was going to come face to face with my mother and I'd pledged to kill her when that meeting occurred.

Could I do it? *Would* I do it? It was my duty as a P.I. but she was family.

Which was more important, family or duty?

I popped the chicken finger into my mouth and chewed it thoughtfully. *I guess I'll find out when the time comes.*

"So you're going to be using Excalibur," Leon said, taking a sip of his soda. "*The* Excalibur."

I nodded. "Yeah, but it's not that impressive; the damned thing's creepy as hell."

My phone rang and the screen displayed the caller ID. Mysterium Import and Export. "Be right back," I told the others as I got up out of the booth and headed outside to take the call. I touched the screen and said, "Harbinger."

"Alec, it's Michael Chester. Are you well?"

"Not too bad," I said, pushing through the door and stepping out into the parking lot. The night seemed to be getting colder every second. "What have you got for me?"

"A possible Cabal member in your area."

"Great, what's their name?"

"I'm afraid it isn't that straightforward, Alec. My contact in the Shadow Watch told me that a couple of his agents are going after this person tomorrow. They want to question him. So I can't just give you his name and let you jeopardize their operation."

I sighed. "So what am I supposed to do?"

"The agents have agreed to let you accompany them when they bring him in. That way you get access to the Cabal member and the Watch get their man."

I thought about it. I hadn't sworn an oath to take down the Midnight Cabal singlehandedly and the agents of the Shadow Watch were sure to know more about what I was getting myself into than I did. Maybe they could help me.

"How does that sound?" Michael asked.

"Fine. How do I contact the agents?"

"You don't. They'll contact you."

Why did I suddenly feel like I was in a spy movie? I sighed frustratedly and said, "Okay, thanks. I'll await their call. Or tape that self-destructs. Or whatever other means they use to contact me."

"Talk soon, Alec." He ended the call.

I went back inside the diner and slid into the booth.

"Any news?" Amy asked.

"Apparently I'm going to be contacted by two Shadow Watch agents and I'm going to accompany them while they catch a Cabal member."

"Shadow Watch?"

"Yeah, I guess you could call them the foot soldiers of the Society of Shadows."

"I thought you were the foot soldiers," she said. "The P.I.s"

"No, not really. It all goes back to when the Society first started and the roles it gave its members. Felicity can probably explain it better than I can." I gestured to Felicity, who was eating an onion ring.

She quickly chewed it and said, "It's simple really. The Society of Shadows was formed in the late 17th Century to fight preternatural threats. At that time, the Midnight Cabal already existed. Its aim was to keep the population enslaved to a growing fear of the supernatural, to engender superstition and terror."

"So who formed the Society?" Amy asked.

"Well, we're not exactly sure," Felicity said.

I took an onion ring and said nothing. I knew the Society had been created by nine witches known as the Coven but that information was hidden even from some high-ranking members.

"The point is," Felicity continued, "the Society put protectors into most cities and towns. These people were known as Wardens. They kept watch in case preternatural danger should arise within their territory. As well as the Wardens, there was a group of Society members tasked with destroying the Midnight Cabal and other paranormal organizations and armies. They were named Templars after the much older organization, the Knights Templar."

She took a sip of soda before continuing. "As time wore on and the world changed, the Society updated itself to keep with the times. The Templars went underground and became known as the Shadow Watch. The Wardens became the Preternatural Investigators that are found in most towns and cities today. Although they have a different name, they still do the same job as the Wardens; keeping the people within their territory safe from supernatural threats."

"And they have cool weapons," Leon added.

"Yes," Felicity said. "And they have cool weapons."

Amy nodded thoughtfully, digesting what she'd just heard. "So all of those unassuming-looking P.I. offices dotted around the country are actually outposts of a secret society?"

"Yeah," I said. "They're the public face of the Society of Shadows."

"Is there a central office somewhere? A headquarters?"

"There is," I said, thinking of the Mysterium Import and Export building in London with its elevator that descended into another realm where the Coven resided.

"And what about the Midnight Cabal?" she asked. "I guess they must have a headquarters too, right? Like an evil lair inside a volcano or something?"

"Probably but it's well-hidden, wherever it is. I doubt it's in this dimension."

Her eyes widened. "Okay, now you're blowing my mind. Are there really other dimensions?"

I took another onion ring and nodded. "I've traveled to three others. I'm sure there are more."

Amy looked into her soda glass wistfully. "Wow, I think I'm in the wrong job."

"Your job is important," I told her. "And the life of a P.I. isn't as glamorous as it may sound."

She took a sip of soda, sighed, and looked out of the window at the cold night. "Just tell me that you're going to get my dad back, Alec."

"I am. As soon as I do what Merlin wants, he'll release your dad and everything will go back to normal."

She leaned in closer over the table. "Will it though? Because if Merlin releases my dad, doesn't that mean he has to go back to the cave again? He's not going to want to do that is he?"

I thought about that for a moment. She was probably right; when Merlin released the Sheriff from the cave, he'd have to go back there himself. Would he renege on the deal and try to stay in our world?

"We'll cross that bridge when we come to it," I told her, uncertain how I could force Merlin back into his prison if he didn't want to go. I had to hope that the wizard followed the faerie code of ethics when it came to deals and oaths.

"What's your plan for tomorrow?" I asked

Felicity in an attempt to steer the conversation in a different direction.

"Well I suppose we're going to have to revisit Lucy Hawthorne," she said. "The other members of the family are innocent as far as magic use goes so that leaves Lucy as our prime suspect."

"You going to knock on her door again?"

She shook her head. "This time we're going to be a bit more devious and put a tail on her when she leaves the house. She has to leave sometime and when she does, we'll be waiting."

"Nice."

"And I want to speak to Charles Hawthorne. He saw something in that smoke that frightened him. I want to know what it was."

"He said he saw the events of the other night when his driver drove the car off the road."

"Well that's not exactly what he said. He mentioned a car wreck. His car wasn't wrecked the other night. I think he was speaking about a different event."

I wasn't convinced. "He could barely string together a coherent sentence, so he probably got his words confused."

"But he didn't mention the demon," Felicity said.

I shrugged. "The demon?"

"The one he saw on the road that night. Merlin said the spell was intended to induce fear in someone. Wouldn't the caster send an image of the demon? Surely that's the most frightful thing Charles has ever seen. But he didn't even mention it. He just said 'the car wreck,' whatever that refers to."

"That doesn't mean he didn't see the demon. It only means he didn't mention it."

"Perhaps," she said but I could see she wasn't convinced.

"It's your case," I told her. "You investigate it any way you want."

"I will." She finished her soda and asked, "What about the Shadow Watch agents you're meeting tomorrow? Do you know when they'll contact you?"

I shook my head. "It's all very cloak and dagger."

"Well maybe we should all get some sleep," she suggested. "Tomorrow is going to be a busy day."

I agreed, albeit reluctantly. I knew I had to get some rest but I felt like a kid who doesn't want to go to bed because they have a test at school the next day. The sooner I closed my eyes tonight, the sooner tomorrow would arrive.

And that meant having to deal with Merlin and the creepy-ass sword in my basement.

7

A loud knocking on my door brought me out of a dream. I jolted upright in bed and blinked against the morning light streaming in through the window. The last vestiges of the dream refused to flee even when faced with the light and remained in my head.

I'd had the same dream before a couple of times. In it, I was standing in an old, abandoned house staring into a full-length mirror. Mallory appeared in the mirror and seemed to be trapped behind the glass. As I gazed into her eyes, her face changed completely, transforming into the visage of a dark-skinned Egyptian woman dressed in a kalasiris, a simple sheath dress worn by women in ancient times.

I slid out of bed and squinted against the light as I peered out of the window. Sheriff Cantrell's patrol car was parked outside, which meant it was Merlin at the door. Not bothering to dress, I went downstairs in my shorts and opened the door.

"Alec," Merlin said as he pushed past me and into the house. "Good to see you. I trust you have a place for us to begin our quest."

"Not yet," I said, padding into the kitchen and putting the coffee machine on. "I'm waiting for a call. You want coffee?"

He nodded. "What call? From whom?"

"I'm not really sure," I said, getting mugs from the cupboard. "A couple of agents from the Shadow Watch."

His eyebrows knitted together. "Shadow Watch?"

"You haven't heard of them, huh? I guess they're a little after your time."

I poured two coffees and gave him one. He sipped it and scrunched his face up. "What sorcery is this?"

"It's called coffee. You said you wanted one."

"Yes, I know what it is from Cantrell's memory and I know he likes it but nothing could prepare me for the taste."

"You'll get used to it."

He sniffed it warily and took another small sip. "Hmm, yes, I think you might be right."

"So," I said. "What do we do while we're waiting for the Watch to get in contact? You want to go home and I'll call you when I hear from them?"

"No, there's no need for that. While we're waiting, you can familiarize yourself with Excalibur."

"I think I'm familiar enough with it already."

"No, you can't be. Not yet anyway. Excalibur isn't just any old sword, Alec. It becomes one with its wielder. Until you let it become part of you, it won't reveal its full potential. And we're going to need its full might for the task at hand."

I took a long sip of my coffee. "I don't like the sound of letting it become part of me. I thought it was supposed to become part of my enemies. When I stab them with it."

"Excalibur and its wielder must become one," he said. "That's how it works. Now, fetch the sword and we'll see how you two get on."

"It's in the basement," I told him. "I have a training area down there."

"Very well, let's go to the basement and put you through your paces."

"I'll get dressed first." I went up to my bedroom and slipped on a pair of jeans and a black T-shirt.

I went back down and rejoined Merlin and then we descended the stairs to the training area. I gestured at the cupboard on the wall. "It's in there."

"Get it out then and I'll judge how well you two work together."

"You make it sound like we're dating." I put my mug of coffee down, opened the cupboard, and took out the sword.

"Wielding Excalibur is not like dating at all," he said. "It's more like a marriage."

As my fingers curled around the grip, I felt a tingling sensation travel through my hand and up along my arm.

"Now strike one of those effigies over there," Merlin said, indicating the training dummies lined up along the wall.

I walked over to the dummies, getting used to the heft of the sword in my hand. It was surprisingly light and comfortable to hold. I positioned myself in front of a dummy and swung Excalibur, aiming for the mass of the chest.

The sword seemed to have other ideas. As it traveled through the air, the blade changed trajectory and sliced into the dummy's neck so forcefully that the dummy's head fell off and rolled across the floor.

"Don't fight the weapon," Merlin advised.

"I'm not fighting it. It's fighting me."

"Become one with the blade. Act in accordance with its wishes."

"No," I said, leaning Excalibur against the wall. "I'm not going to use a sword that does its own thing."

Merlin frowned as if he didn't understand my protest. "Isn't cutting off your enemy's head preferable to hitting them in the chest? The most expedient attack is a swift kill."

"I get to decide that," I told him. "Not the sword."

He tapped his forefinger against his lips thoughtfully. "Hmm, I can see we're going to have some teething problems."

"There won't be any problems as long as the sword goes where I want it to."

He tutted. "That isn't how Excalibur works." He walked over the rack of weapons on the wall. "These weapons you have here are simply inert pieces of metal. They are tools to be used how you see fit. Excalibur isn't simply a piece of forged steel; it's a living thing. It isn't your tool; it's your companion."

I looked at the sword leaning innocuously against the wall. There was no way I was going to wield a weapon that had a mind of its own. "I'll pass. I have plenty of good swords already. You can take that one back."

Merlin arched an eyebrow amusedly. "That isn't possible, Alec. You made a pledge to the Lady of the Lake and she gifted you the sword so that you may carry out that pledge. You can't go back on it now."

"I don't want to go back on the pledge," I told him, even though I'd give anything right now to be able to travel back in time to that moment at the pool and keep my dumb mouth closed. "I just don't need the sword, thanks."

"It isn't an option. The Midnight Cabal killed the Lady of the Lake's sister. You will use Excalibur, which the Lady of the Lake has given you, to destroy them. It's simple. I don't understand why you're resisting."

"Because no one mentioned anything about living swords or steel companions."

"Don't fret, my friend. These are early days. Arthur was just the same when he first tried to wield Excalibur. But later, when he and the sword became one, he used its power to carve out his kingdom."

"I'm not really into the whole kingdom thing."

"Nevertheless, you will use Excalibur to fight against the Midnight Cabal. Now, pick up the sword and attack another of the effigies."

I sighed and took Excalibur's grip lightly in my hand. "I won't have any effigies left if the sword keeps decapitating them."

A knock at the door saved me having to destroy another dummy. I put down the sword and said, "I should see who that is."

Leaving him in the basement, I went up and opened the front door. A young Asian woman stood outside, dressed in a long black coat that reached to her ankles. She nodded at me by way of a greeting. "Alec Harbinger, I'm Honoka Chan. The guy in the car is my partner, Todd Benson."

A black SUV sat on the street, engine running. The blonde guy behind the wheel stared at me with the same expression a scientist might have when examining a germ through a microscope.

"We were told you wanted a ride-along," Honoka said.

"That's right."

She nodded toward the car. "Come on, let's go."

"Wait a second, there's someone else coming too," I told her. "Turning to face the basement steps, I shouted, "Sheriff, our ride is here."

Merlin bounded up the steps as quickly as Cantrell's body allowed. When he saw Honoka at the door, he performed a short bow that just seemed weird. "Allow me to introduce myself. I am—"

"Sheriff John Cantrell," she finished for him. "Widower. One daughter, Amy. Wife killed in a church massacre that has probable paranormal connections."

"Great," I said, "We all know each other. Let's go."

Honoka held up a hand. "You can come. The sheriff stays here."

"He's with me," I said. "He's helping me on a case."

"We agreed to take you, Harbinger. No one

else."

"But I'm the sheriff," Merlin said.

"I don't care if you're Merlin the magician, you're not coming with us."

"Well actually…" he began.

"He'll wait here," I said quickly.

Honoka turned away from the door and walked across the lawn to the SUV. "Time to go, Harbinger. Say your goodbyes."

"Wait here," I told Merlin. "I'll be back soon."

"But I wanted to come too."

"They won't let you in the car."

He looked at the SUV and then back at me. "All right. I see what you mean."

"I shouldn't be too long," I said. "Just make yourself at home until I get back. Watch TV or something."

"Okay," he said loudly, "I'll just stay here and watch TV." He shot me a knowing smile.

"What are you doing?"

"Letting them know that I'm staying here."

"They know that already." I stepped out onto the stoop.

"Okay, Alec, see you soon." He was speaking loudly again. As he closed the front door, he tapped his nose and winked at me.

As I walked to the SUV, I wondered if it was safe to leave Merlin alone in my house.

I climbed into the back of the vehicle and closed the door.

"The sheriff's weird," Honoka said from the passenger seat.

"I can't argue with that," I said.

Todd Benson turned around in the driver's seat to look at me. "Hey, man, I'm Todd." He held out his hand.

I shook it. He tried to crush my hand but I gave as good as I got. I wasn't into machismo bullshit but I wasn't going to let him assert any dominance over me either.

"Okay, let's go." Spinning back around in his seat, he put the car into Drive and pulled away from the curb.

"Where are we going?" I asked.

"We're going to pick up this man," Honoka said, passing a photograph to me. It showed a fair-haired man in his thirties loading sacks of groceries into the back of a station wagon. He wore thick-rimmed glasses and a tan jacket and looked totally average in every way.

"Who is he?" I asked.

"Gerald Garland," Honoka said, taking the photo back. "We're fairly sure he's involved with the Cabal albeit in a minor way. He's strictly small time, an amateur occultist who thinks he can run with the big dogs so we're not real interested in him per se but he probably has information we can use to infiltrate higher levels of the organization."

"Guys like him roll over pretty easily and give up their friends real fast when the pressure's on," Todd said.

"And how do you two put the pressure on?"

Todd smirked. "Stick around and you'll find out. What's your interest in the Cabal anyway? I thought you P.I. guys just caught ghosts and handled the occasional werewolf."

Although professional pride made me want to educate this Shadow Watch agent regarding the important role of the Preternatural Investigator, I resisted the temptation. I had a feeling Honoka and Todd knew a lot about me.

If Honoka's summary of Sheriff Cantrell's life was anything to go by, she and Todd had done their research before coming to Dearmont. They probably knew all the cases I'd worked on, the events in Paris and my subsequent relocation to Maine. They definitely knew who my father was and the fact that he was missing. They might even think he was a traitor who'd defected to the Cabal.

"Don't forget we're a big hit at Halloween parties," I said.

He snorted. "Yeah, right, dude. Seriously, though, things must be real quiet around here, am I right? I mean, if you want real preternatural action in this part of the country, you need to go to Massachusetts."

"Or Vermont," Honoka added.

Todd frowned at her. "Vermont? What the hell is in Vermont?"

"Remember that witch cult we busted?"

His face lit up. "Oh yeah, Vermont is wild, man!"

In an attempt to distract myself from their chatter, I watched the buildings on Main Street pass by the window. As we drove out of town and onto the highway, the buildings disappeared and were replaced by an endless procession of trees.

"Hey, Alec," Todd said after we'd been on the highway for half an hour. "You're real quiet back there. Don't you have anything to ask us? I bet you haven't met anyone from the Shadow Watch before. You must have a thousand questions."

"No, not really."

"Oh." He concentrated intently on the road for a couple of minutes, during which time he was either fighting his disappointment in my lack of interest or trying to think of something else to say.

It turned out to be the latter when he said, "Because we don't mind if you want to ask us anything. You might want to know about what weapons we use or what tactics we use. You know, because we're, like, cool and stuff."

"No, I'm good."

He fell into a sullen silence after that. For maybe five minutes. Then, out of the blue, he asked, "Hey, Harbinger, have you ever heard of something called the Melandra Codex?"

Honoka shot him a look and shook her head at him almost imperceptibly.

Todd shrugged at her innocently and said, "Fine, I'll shut up."

It was obvious Todd had said something he shouldn't have and since my only other form of entertainment was watching the trees roll past, I leaned forward and said. "No, I haven't heard of the Melandra Codex. What is it?"

"Nothing," Honoka said with a note of finality.

"Todd?" I asked.

"Nothing," he said, sounding like a scolded child.

I sat back in the seat and took out my phone. I sent a text to Felicity.

What is the Melandra Codex?

The reply came back a couple of minutes later.

No idea. Why?

Not important right now, I texted back before putting the phone away.

But it was obvious from Honoka's wordless reprimand that it *was* important. Why had Todd asked me about it? After all, in his eyes, I was just a lowly P.I. who caught ghosts and dealt with the occasional werewolf.

Retrieving the phone from my pocket again, I typed "Melandra Codex" into the search engine. There were no results.

"Turn here," Honoka told Todd. He did as instructed and guided the SUV onto a track that led to a farmhouse.

As we bumped along the track, Honoka turned to me and said, "You wait in the car while we go in and get the guy."

"Sure."

We reached the farmhouse and Todd

applied the brakes, bringing us to a stop next to a battered blue Toyota.

The two agents left the vehicle and split up, Honoka going around back while Todd approached the front door. He knocked and waited. When there was no answer, he called, "Gerald Garland, you in there?"

After receiving no answer a second time, he kicked the door open and slipped inside.

A few moments later, Gerald Garland burst out of the house and sprinted for the trees. I had no idea where Todd or Honoka were so I opened my door and pursued the fleeing man into the woods.

He was easy to track as he crashed through the undergrowth and branches and I soon caught up with him. I tackled him to the ground and we both rolled in the dirt. Before he could regain his feet, I pinned one of his arms behind his back and dragged him to his feet.

"Ow!" he said, "There's no need for that. I'm willing to talk to you guys."

"Of course you are. That's why you came bursting out of the house like Justin Gatlin." I shoved him in the direction of the farmhouse.

"You can't blame me for trying. I wasn't

going to just roll over and let them take me. I suppose you want to know all about my involvement with the Midnight Cabal. Well I won't talk and you can't make me."

"I'm not going to make you," I said, pointing to Honoka and Todd, who were emerging from the house. "They are."

He looked at them and grimaced. "Who are they?"

I was probably supposed to say, "Your worst nightmare," or something equally dramatic but instead I just said, "Two people who want to talk to you."

"What's with the coats? They look like they're in a Matrix movie or something."

"I don't know."

"They're not going to hurt me are they?"

I remembered Todd's crushing handshake. "I wouldn't count on them going easy on you."

"Listen," he said, stopping in his tracks. "I'll talk to you, okay? I know you. I don't know them."

"You don't know me."

"Alec, I'm an occultist. Do you really think I wouldn't know who the dashing local P.I. is? You've been in the newspaper and on TV. You're a local hero."

"I'm no hero."

Todd was now standing by the SUV, looking impatient. He shouted to me. "Come on, man, don't stand there shooting the shit with the guy. Bring him over here."

Gerald looked at me with a worried expression. "Alec, please, I'm begging you. Don't make me go with them. I haven't done anything wrong. I got involved with the wrong crowd, that's all."

"How?" I asked him. "How did you get involved with the Midnight Cabal? How did you first make contact with them?"

"If I tell you, will you help me out?"

I wasn't sure how I could possibly help him. If I let him go and he fled into the woods, the two agents would catch him easily. "I can't help you, Gerald, it's too late for that."

I heard a vehicle approaching and looked in that direction to see a police cruiser making its way along the track to the farmhouse.

"Oh, thank God!" Gerald exclaimed, "It's the police!"

I could see Merlin sitting behind the cruiser's steering wheel, a mischievous grin on his face.

I let out a long sigh.

Gerald took the opportunity to run forward, pulling his arm out of my grasp. "Sheriff! Sheriff, I'm being harassed!" He bolted for the cruiser.

Merlin had parked next to the SUV and was getting out of the car.

Todd began sprinting toward Gerald to block him before he reached the sheriff. He tackled Gerald to the ground in much the same way I'd taken him down in the woods. But instead of letting Gerald get back to his feet, Todd sat on his chest and pinned his wrists.

"Sheriff, help!" Gerald shouted.

Merlin took in the scene in front of him, said something under his breath, and flicked his hands forward. Todd, Gerald, and Honoka froze. I don't mean they were covered in ice or anything like that; they simply stopped moving.

I continued walking out of the woods. At least he hadn't frozen me along with everyone else.

When Merlin saw me, he asked, "What in the name of Cernunnos is going on here, Alec?"

"More to the point," I countered, "What the hell are you doing here?"

"Aha!" he said, smiling. "I understood your

message at the front door."

"What message?"

"You said I couldn't come in *their* car. Your unspoken message was obvious; you wanted me to follow in *my* car."

"There was no message. I wanted you to stay at home."

His face fell. "Oh." Then he brightened again. "Well it looks like I came at the right time. There's all manner of chaos happening here. Who is this fellow?" He pointed at Gerald, whose motionless mouth was open as he shouted soundlessly for help.

"That's Gerald Garland. He has some connection with the Cabal."

"And remind me who these two are again." He gestured to Todd and Honoka.

"Todd Benson and Honoka Chan. Agents of the Shadow Watch. They want to question Gerald about his involvement with the Cabal, see if they can get him to tell them other names higher up in the ranks."

He thought about that for a moment, touching his finger to his lips as he looked from Gerald to Todd and then to Honoka. "And why are we aligning ourselves with these people?"

"It's the only way we could get to a Cabal member quickly."

"And what makes you think they would share any information they got from this man with you, Alec?"

"We're all on the same team" I said. "At least we were until you came along and zapped them. Now they're just going to be pissed at me."

He stepped forward and put a hand on Todd's head. Then he made a gesture with his other hand and closed his eyes. "This man's intent has nothing to do with sharing information with you. He didn't invite you to join him so that he could share information with you; he wanted to question you." He frowned. "Something about your father."

I should have known the Shadow Watch would take this opportunity to ask me about my father. As I'd guessed in the car on the way over here, they probably thought he was a traitor and that I knew where he was.

Merlin took his hand from Todd's head and walked over to Honoka. He placed his hand on her head, closed his eyes, and repeated the magical gesture. "She had the same intent as her partner; to question you about your father." Removing his hand and opening his eyes, he added, "All of this was nothing more than a ruse, Alec. You were allowed to participate in this bust only so they could gain your trust and later question you."

"Like I'd tell them anything," I said.

"If they couldn't learn anything from you by pretending to be your friends, they had further plans."

"Oh? What were they?"

He went to the SUV and opened the tailgate. Reaching inside, he picked up something and brought it over to me. "They were going to use this."

The object in his hand was something I'd seen before and never wanted to see again; an enchanted iron collar used by the Spanish Inquisition to extract confessions from heretics. I'd been forced to wear one of these collars before, when the Society questioned me about the events in Paris. The magic infusing the collar forced the wearer to tell the truth when questioned.

"So, Alec, what is your plan now?" Merlin asked.

Looking over the scene in front of me, I

said, "Can you unfreeze Gerald but leave these two as they are?"

He nodded. "I can but the spell only lasts a short while. The agents will regain movement and thought again soon."

"How soon?"

"Fifteen minutes or so."

"That's long enough."

He flicked his hand at Gerald and muttered a few indistinct words. Gerald continued the shout that had been cut off by the spell. "Sheriff! Sheriff, help!" He realized that Todd was immobile and let out a short scream before wriggling his way out from beneath the Shadow agent.

As he stood up and brushed dirt off his clothes, he saw Merlin and me standing by the SUV. In that split second, he looked like he might flee into the trees again.

"Don't even think about it, Gerald," I said.

His eyes darted from Todd to Honoka. "What happened to them?"

"That isn't important," I told him. "What *is* important is that if you tell me how you made contact with the Cabal, I'm going to let you go. But we don't have long before the spell wears off and they wake up."

"Okay," he said, nodding. "Just give me a head start, that's all I need."

"Give me a name or a location and you get about fifteen minutes before they come after you."

"There's a meeting place," he said. "In Rockport. A house near the harbor."

"How did you find out about it?"

"A chatroom called The Emerald Tablet. That's where they recruit members." He looked at Todd and Honoka and then at the battered blue Toyota. "Please, I've told you everything I know. Now let me go."

"You haven't told me the address of the house in Rockport."

He gave me the address and then ran for the car. The engine roared into life and the wheels kicked up dirt before the Toyota lurched forward and sped toward the track.

"Well that was most productive," Merlin said happily.

I watched the Toyota disappear into the distance and ran over what I'd just learned from Gerald in my head.

The address he'd given me was Lucy Hawthorne's.

8

Felicity stopped her Mini at the gate of the Hawthorne residence and waited for the security guard to appear from the red brick booth.

She'd spent most of last night thinking about Charles Hawthorne's words regarding a car wreck and she was still sure he hadn't been referring to the night his driver had driven the car off the road.

She accepted Alec's theory that Charles might have made a mistake due to being drunk but she wanted to be sure. The only way to do that was to question the man now that he'd hopefully sobered up.

"Do you think he'll let us in?" Leon asked from the passenger seat.

"I know he specifically hired Alec," she said, "But I can't think of any reason why he wouldn't want to speak to us."

"I can think of a couple of reasons," Leon said.

The guard appeared from the booth, eyes hidden behind sunglasses. He leaned down to Felicity's window and adjusted his head so that he was looking at her over the top of the glasses. "What can I do for you today?"

"We're here to see Charles Hawthorne," she told him.

"Is that right? I'm pretty sure he isn't expecting any visitors today. And we're on a lockdown after some trouble last night."

"Yes, we know all about that, we were here. If you could just tell him that Felicity Lake and Leon Smith are here, I'm sure he'll want to talk to us."

He arched his eyebrows incredulously. "In regard to what? Mr Hawthorne is a busy man."

"Tell him we're from Harbinger P.I."

Letting out a short laugh, he said, "I'm pretty sure Mr Hawthorne doesn't want to talk to any ghost hunters."

"All right," Felicity said, deciding to end this game right now. "Tell Mr Hawthorne that two associates from Harbinger P.I. came by to see him today and you told us to leave without even checking with him if he wanted to see us. I wonder how happy he'll be about that."

"Okay, okay," he said. "Wait here." Letting out a sigh, he sauntered to his booth and disappeared inside.

The guard didn't reappear but a couple of minutes after he'd entered the booth, the gate clicked and swung open.

"Nice work," Leon said.

"Thanks." She put the Mini into gear and drove along the driveway to the parking area. The mansion sat silently in the cold sunlight. A blonde man with a ponytail was out front washing a black Bentley with soapy water. The peaceful scene was a world away from the chaos of last night.

Felicity parked next to a silver Rolls Royce and climbed out of the car. Leon joined her and together they walked to the front door, which was already open. The butler appeared in the foyer and looked taken aback when he saw them.

"Oh," he said. "The security guard said someone from Harbinger P.I. was here. I assumed it was Mr Harbinger himself. That's the message I relayed to Mr Hawthorne."

"We're working on the case," Felicity told him. She thought it prudent not to mention that she'd actually taken over the case from Alec. "We'd like to see Mr Hawthorne now, please."

"One moment," the butler said. He disappeared through a door at the far end of the foyer.

When he reappeared, he beckoned them to follow him and led them to a brightly lit room at the rear of the house that looked out over the garden. Charles was sitting in his wheelchair, staring out of the window. When Felicity and Leon entered, he spun around to face them, his face like thunder.

"I'm paying your boss good money to work on this case so why is he sending two lackeys around to my house? Where is he?"

"I'm Felicity Lake and this is Leon Smith. We are associates of Mr Harbinger. He's currently busy so we've come here to ask you a couple of questions about last night."

"Ask me questions? I thought you were the ones who were supposed to have the answers. I should be asking *you* questions. Like what the hell was that damned smoke and where did it come from?"

"That's what we've come to talk to you about," Felicity said. "Last night, you said you saw a car wreck in the smoke. Can you tell me more about that?"

He looked at her like she was crazy. "What are you talking about? I didn't say anything like that."

"Yes, you did," she said, realizing this interview wasn't going to get her anywhere. Was Charles Hawthorne just being annoying on purpose or was he trying to hide something?

"Get out of my house," he said. "You're supposed to be finding out who's doing this to me, not asking me foolish questions about car wrecks." He pressed a button on the arm of the wheelchair. "Wesley, our guests are leaving."

Wesley came into the room and swept his arm toward the door. "This way, please."

Felicity knew there was no point in protesting. Without a word to Charles Hawthorne, she left the room with Leon. The butler showed them to the front door and closed it behind them after they'd stepped outside into the chilly air.

ADAM J WRIGHT

"We should have known that wouldn't end well," Leon said as they crossed the gravel parking area to the Mini. As they passed the black Bentley that was being washed, he paused and said, "Wait a minute, all might not be lost. That guy washing the car is Jonas, Charles's driver. If Charles was involved in a car wreck, Jonas would know about it, right?"

"It's worth a try," Felicity said.

They approached the blonde, pony-tailed man. Leon said, "Hey, it's Jonas, isn't it?"

The man nodded. "I know you. You are Brad's friend." He had an accent that Felicity placed as Slovakian.

"Yeah, that's right," Leon said. "My name's Leon and this is my friend Felicity."

Jonas nodded to her.

"I was just wondering," Leon said casually. "Have you been working here long?"

"Exactly one year," Jonas said. "Mr Hawthorne hired me the day after the Fall party last year."

"That's cool. I bet you're a careful driver, right?"

"Very careful. Of course."

"Me too. But sometimes it doesn't matter how careful you are, you get involved in an accident that isn't even your fault. You know what I mean? There are some crazy people on the roads. That ever happen to you? It happens to me a lot."

"Crazy people, yes. Accidents not so much."

"But you were run off the road the other night, weren't you? I heard about that."

Jonas nodded. "Yes. Drunk driver. Very crazy."

Felicity knew that Charles Hawthorne's official story of the accident was that Jonas had swerved to avoid a drunk driver heading straight for them. Obviously Jonas was sticking to that version of events.

"That the worse thing that ever happened to you?" Leon asked. "I was involved in a car wreck once when I wrapped my Porsche around a tree. Anything like that ever happen to you?"

Jonas shook his head earnestly. "No. No car wrecks ever. I was run off the road by…the drunken driver…and that was the worst that ever happened to me."

"Cool," Leon said. "Hey, good talking to you. Take care."

Jonas nodded at them both and resumed his work.

When they were both inside the Mini, Felicity said, "So if Jonas is to be believed, there hasn't been a car wreck in the last year. At least not one when he was at the wheel. Of course, he might be lying. He's lying about the other night, saying what Charles told him to say."

"Yeah, but he's hardly going to mention a demon to two people he doesn't know."

"True, but he's also not going to mention a car wreck if Charles told him to keep quiet about it." She started the engine. "There has to have been a car wreck. Why would someone attack Charles Hawthorne with an illusion spell and make him see a vision of one?"

"Yeah, that would be crazy," Leon said. "And at the party, didn't Charles say he didn't want to see it again? So that must mean he's seen it before."

The gate opened as they approached it and Felicity drove past the guard's booth. When she reached the end of the driveway, but before she joined the traffic on the highway, she pulled over and took her phone out of her handbag.

A quick search of car accidents in the area revealed only one major incident last year. "This is interesting," she said, showing Leon a photo of a crumpled car. The picture was part of an article that described an accident that had killed a young man and injured two other people.

"Did that happen around here?" Leon asked.

Felicity nodded. "Not far from here. It happened last year. On the same night as Jane Hawthorne's Fall party."

9

"This is it," I told Merlin. "Pull over here."

He pulled the police cruiser over and killed the engine. We were about fifty yards from Lucy Hawthorne's house, far enough away to not look too conspicuous.

"Are we going to go and confront her?" he asked.

"I am" I said. "You're going to wait here. And there's no unspoken message in what I'm saying. I really want you to stay in the car."

"But why? If she's a member of the Cabal, you may need my help. You don't have Excalibur to hand."

"No, but I have this." I showed him the enchanted dagger I'd taken from Todd and Honoka's SUV."

"That knife is no Excalibur."

"No, it isn't but that's probably a good thing. I'm not going to kill Lucy, just talk to her. If her house is used as a Cabal meeting place, she probably has a wealth of information we can use to infiltrate their organization."

"And how will you extract that information from her? I have a number of spells that—"

"Just leave this to me, okay?" I got out of the car and slid the dagger into the back of my jeans. It wasn't raining like the last time I was here but a strong breeze was tossing the dead leaves around the street. Before I closed the car door, I leaned in and reiterated to Merlin, "Don't leave the car."

He sighed. "Very well, I will await your return."

I closed the door and walked the fifty yards to Lucy's house with my hands in my pockets. Wearing only the T-shirt and jeans I'd had on when Honoka had knocked at my door earlier, I felt chilled to the bone.

The large federal style house looked empty as I approached the porch. There weren't any lights on that I could see. The windows were like empty black eye sockets.

I stepped onto the porch and rapped the

front door knocker three times to announce my presence.

I wasn't expecting an answer. I was prepared to go around back and break into the house. So I was surprised when I heard movement and then the sound of someone drawing back the bolt on the inside of the door. It opened a crack and a young woman's face appeared. She looked me over and smiled shyly. "You're Alec Harbinger."

"I am. And you're Lucy Hawthorne, I presume."

"You presume correctly." She opened the door fully. "You must be freezing out there. Come in."

"Thanks." I stepped inside. The house was warm. Lucy was a petite redhead with a slight resemblance to her brother and sister in her features. She was dressed casually in jeans and a T-shirt that had the words *Miskatonic University* across the chest. I had the same T-shirt at home and knew that written across the back were the words *Department of Medieval Metaphysics*.

"Just go through there and I'll bring coffee," she said, indicating a door on my left.

Unsure why she seemed to be expecting me

and how she knew who I was, I stepped through the door and into a cozy living room. A fire blazed in a marble fireplace and the pleasant smell of cedar wood lingered on the air. One wall was completely covered in bookshelves holding what must have been thousands of paperbacks.

In one corner, a computer, keyboard, and dozens of notebooks littered the surface of a large mahogany desk.

A sofa and two easy chairs were arranged around a coffee table whose wooden legs were carved into tentacles.

Lucy came in and set a tray down on the table. There was a pot of coffee, two mugs, a pitcher of cream, and packets of sugar. "Help yourself," she said. "And take a seat anywhere you like."

This friendly woman was a world away from the introverted recluse Charles Hawthorne had described to me.

I sat on the sofa and felt something pressing into my back. "Don't be alarmed," I said. "I just have to put this on the table." I took the dagger out of my jeans and placed it on the coffee table.

Lucy didn't seem phased at all that I'd come

into her house with a weapon. "No problem," she said. "Just a tool of your trade."

"You don't seem surprised that I'm here," I said.

"Should I be?" She poured coffee from the pot into both of the mugs. "Help yourself to cream and sugar."

"Did someone tell you I was coming here?"

"Brad called me last night and told me something weird had happened at the party. He knows I'm interested in that kind of thing. He also told me that you were there and you were asking about me." She added cream to her coffee and stirred it.

"And I came here yesterday," I told her. "You probably saw me in the car outside."

She frowned. "No, I wasn't here yesterday. I was at a bookstore in Boston doing a book signing. Then I had dinner with my agent. I stayed at a hotel. I didn't get home until this morning."

I remembered the face peering through the curtains at me yesterday. "Do you live alone?"

"Yes."

"When I came by yesterday, I thought I saw someone in the house."

Lucy shook her head. "No, that isn't possible."

"Have you checked the house since you came home?"

"I have an alarm. I turned it on when I left for Boston and I turned it off when I got back. No one has been in the house."

Maybe my eyes had been playing tricks on me yesterday.

"So," Lucy said. "What's happening back home? And why has Dad hired a preternatural investigator? It sounds exciting. It almost makes me wish I was still living there."

"I understand you and your family don't have much contact."

"No, not really. Dad and I don't see eye to eye on most things. Well, just about anything, really. I still send Brad my books. And he called me last night, as I already mentioned."

"What did he tell you?"

"That there was some kind of smoke that appeared from nowhere and everyone ran outside. And you and two other people had glowing swords. Do you mind if I put that scene into one of my books?"

"I guess not. The thing is, Lucy, I'm trying to track down the person responsible for sending that smoke to the house. At your father's request, I checked out your mother and Brad and Elise."

"What? He thinks one of us did it? Typical."

"When he hired me, he did express the opinion that a member of the family might be responsible for some recent attacks he's experienced."

She looked surprised. "What kind of attacks?"

"Before I go into that, I want to ask you a question."

"Okay."

"What do you know about the Midnight Cabal?"

Her eyes went wide with excitement. "Oh my God, you've heard of them too. I thought I was the only one who knew." '

"Knew what?"

"Wait here." She left the room hurriedly and returned with a thick reference book. Placing it on the coffee table, she opened it to a chapter that was headed *Secret Societies*.

"I was researching old secret societies for a novel I'm writing and I came across this mention of the Midnight Cabal. It says they were around hundreds of years ago but probably disappeared sometime around 1745. Now, you see this magic circle symbol?" She pointed to a diagram in the book. I recognized the symbol; the last time I'd seen it was on a pin my mother was wearing. "That's the symbol of the Cabal."

She closed the book. "Here's the weird part. I've seen that symbol cropping up every now and then in a chatroom."

"The Emerald Tablet," I said.

"Yes! You know it!"

"I've heard of it."

"Here's what I think. I think the Midnight Cabal didn't disappear in 1745 at all. I think it's still operating today."

"Because of a symbol in a chatroom?"

"Not only that. There are other things too. There's some evidence that the Cabal may have been carrying out secret projects during World War Two."

"Evidence?"

"Documents that have come to light recently. Even some photos. Yes, I know that stuff can be faked and I know there are a million conspiracy theories on the Net but this looks real."

While she talked, I wondered why Gerald

Garland had told me this house was being used as a Cabal meeting place. Lucy seemed to be no more than an enthusiastic conspiracy theorist.

"Lucy, do you know a man named Gerald Garland?"

"Yes, of course. Mainemagicman423."

"What?"

"That's his username on the Emerald Tablet. I'm Lucy Loreless. Like the actress. But instead of L A W L E S S, it's spelled *L O R E* L E S S. Get it?"

"Yeah, I get it. Has Gerald been around here? To the house?"

"A couple of times."

"He told me you hold meetings here."

She nodded. "That's right."

"Lucy, he told me they were Midnight Cabal meetings."

Her hand flew to her mouth and her eyes widened even more. "What? No. How could he...?"

"What did you discuss at those meetings?"

"We talked about the Midnight Cabal, of course. I explained why I thought they still existed today. But we discussed other things as well. Occult studies. Secret societies like the

Cabal, yes, but also other groups like the Golden Dawn and the Illuminati."

I took a deep breath and released it slowly. I'd been on a wild goose chase. It was now apparent that Charles Hawthorne's belief that someone in his family was attacking him was nothing more than paranoia. Someone was using magic against him but it wasn't any of his family members.

And Gerald Garland's assertion that this address was a Cabal meeting place was nothing more than a misunderstanding on his part. He'd believed that the like-minded occultists and conspiracy theorists he'd met here were members of the Cabal.

That was the trouble with secret societies; they were so secret that anyone could misinterpret an innocent situation—like talking to fellow enthusiasts—as being part of the society's activities and there was no way to verify or debunk that belief.

That meant I was back to square one as far as the Midnight Cabal was concerned. Merlin wasn't going to be happy about that.

At least I could give Felicity some information to help her investigation into the Hawthorne case, namely that Lucy was nothing more than an armchair occultist. She'd been genuinely surprised when I'd mentioned the attacks on her father.

"Thanks for the coffee," I said, getting up.

"You're welcome. Listen, could I ask you a favor? Would it be possible for me to interview you some time? I think talking to you would give me some great material for a book."

"Maybe," I said, picking up my dagger from the coffee table.

"Great! I have a card here somewhere." She went to the desk and rummaged through the papers until she found a business card. Handing it to me, she said, "Call me sometime and let me know when you have some free time."

I slid the card into my back pocket and said, "I will."

She saw me to the door and as I stepped out, she gave me a little wave. "Nice meeting you."

"You too," I said.

She closed the door and I walked along the street to the police cruiser. Merlin had fallen asleep, his head lolling back against the headrest.

I got in and shook him.

Bleary-eyed, he squinted against the daylight and asked, "Did you force her to talk?"

"No," I told him. "She isn't a member of the Cabal at all. She isn't responsible for the attacks on Charles Hawthorne either."

He huffed. "Well that's just great. Now we don't have any leads at all."

"That's correct."

"So what do we do now?"

"I don't know about you but I'm calling it a day."

"Perhaps you could train with Excalibur some more."

"No, not today. I've had enough of that sword for the moment. And since we're no closer to finding the Cabal, it doesn't look like I'll have to use it anytime soon anyway."

"All right," he conceded. "I'll take you home."

During the drive back to Dearmont, we were both silent. I was wondering if I was going to catch a break and be able to fund some useful nugget of information in my search for the Cabal. I just hoped Felicity was having more luck with the Hawthorne case.

As for Merlin, I had no idea what thoughts were running through his mind.

He dropped me off outside my house and as

I got out of the car, he said, "Shall I pick you up in the morning?"

"No," I said. "I'll call you if I get any leads. It may take some time."

"This isn't progressing as I'd hoped, Alec."

"Welcome to the world of a P.I." I closed the car door and ambled up the driveway to my house. Merlin honked his horn and waved at me as he drove away but I ignored him. Something had set my senses on edge.

I had magical wards set up around the house and along the street that warned me if anyone with ill intent passed through them. I guessed that Todd and Honoka had disabled the wards earlier because if they hadn't—and their intent was ill as Merlin had detected—the wards would have warned me.

So that meant the feeling of anxiousness I was experiencing right now as I walked toward my front door was purely a gut instinct. Removing the dagger from my jeans, I unlocked the door and entered the house.

The first thing I noticed was a smell that seemed to be a mixture of rotting earth and blood. I couldn't detect where it was coming from as it seemed to permeate the entire house.

There was also an atmospheric change, like

the feeling that lingers in the air after a thunderstorm.

I stood still and listened for a sound that might give away an intruder. I heard nothing out of the ordinary.

Maybe you're imagining it. You're just tired.

I'm not imagining that smell.

I went down to the basement and checked the training area. Nothing seemed out of order. Excalibur was leaning against the wall where I'd left it. I went back upstairs and checked the first floor. Again, nothing seemed amiss. If there was someone—or something—in the house, they hadn't been down here. They were upstairs.

I went up carefully and quietly, the dagger held loosely in my grip but ready for action should I need it.

The smell was stronger up here.

The first room I came to was my bedroom. The door was open, exactly as I'd left it earlier. I slipped into the room and was greeted with a sight that shocked me.

Lying on the floor in front of the full-length mirror was a woman. Dirt caked her body and face. Her hair was matted and plastered to her head, neck and shoulders. Her naked body was covered with bloody scratches and wounds. She lay in a fetal position, knees drawn up to her face, her arms wrapped around her legs. I wasn't sure if she was dead or alive.

Crouching next to her, I placed a finger against her neck to check for a pulse. Relief flooded through me when I felt one, steady and strong. I touched her shoulder. "Hey, can you hear me?"

She shifted slightly and whispered something weakly. The sound was too thin for me to hear what she was saying.

I leaned closer to her face.

She whispered again.

"Alec."

Turning toward me, she reached up and put her arms around me, pulling herself up so that her eyes looked into mine.

"Alec."

Now I recognized her. With a flood of emotion, I pulled her close to me and held her, whispering her name.

"Mallory."

10

I led Mallory to the bathroom. She leaned on me heavily, saying nothing more now that I knew who she was. I helped her into the shower and turned on the water before saying, "I'll give you some privacy. I'll be right outside the door."

"No." She shook her head, her eyes wild. "Stay."

"Okay."

She leaned against the tiles and let the hot water sluice the dirt away. As the grime disappeared and the wounds on her body were revealed in greater detail, I could see that they weren't straight slashes like a knife might leave but looked more like jagged claw marks. They ran across her arms, stomach, and legs.

Opening the bathroom cabinet, I took out antiseptic cream and an assortment of bandages and Band-Aids. From what I could see, the wounds weren't deep enough to require stitches. I got the impression that Mallory was suffering more from mental anguish than from physical pain.

If she'd come into the house through the mirror in my bedroom, as it appeared she'd done, then she'd probably come from Shadow Land. That place wasn't good for anyone's state of mind.

She spent at least twenty minutes under the shower and when she was done, she came out looking a million times better than she had when she'd gone in there.

I handed her a towel and she dried herself quickly. Then she used the bandages to dress her wounds.

"Mallory, are you okay? You don't have to talk if you don't want to. I just want to know that you're all right."

She nodded. "I'm okay, Alec. I've just been alone for so long that I've forgotten the art of conversation" When she was finished with the bandages, she asked, "How long have I been gone?"

"About three months."

"It feels like ten years."

"Were you in Shadow Land?"

She nodded, her face becoming grim. "I discovered his lair was located there and I found a way to follow him. But I got trapped and I couldn't find a way out."

"Until you came through my mirror just now."

"There's a spell Mister Scary uses to travel back and forth between Shadow Land and our world. I learned it over time and when I finally used it, I managed to break through into your bedroom." Her face contorted as she tried to hold back tears but they burst forth despite her efforts. She threw her arms around me and wept.

I held her and said, "It's good to have you back."

"There's so much I have to tell you," she said. "But I'm so tired."

"Do you want to sleep?"

She nodded.

I led her into the bedroom and pulled back the comforter on the bed. She slid beneath it and placed her head on the pillow.

"I'll be downstairs," I told her. "If you need anything, call out and I'll come running."

"I just need to sleep. I haven't felt safe for so long."

"You're safe now." I closed the curtains to block out the light coming in through the window. When I turned back to face the bed, Mallory was asleep.

Quietly, I went downstairs and sat in the easy chair in the living room. If Mallory needed me for anything, I'd be able to hear her from here.

I took out my phone and called Felicity.

She answered after a couple of rings. "Hello, Alec."

"Hi, how's it going?"

"We went to speak to Charles Hawthorne today and he was very rude. I'm in the office with Leon doing some research."

"Cool. Listen, I met Lucy Hawthorne today. She's not our attacker. I'll explain everything later but I need you to do a favor for me before you come home."

"All right. What is it?"

"Can you pick up some clothing that would fit Mallory?"

"Mallory? Is she there?"

"Yeah."

"What does she need?"

"Everything."

"Is she all right?"

"I don't know," I said truthfully. "She's been trapped in Shadow Land for months and she escaped by coming through my bedroom mirror."

"I'll go to the store right away."

"There's no hurry. She's sleeping at the moment."

"Still, she could wake up anytime. Leon can hold the fort here while I go shopping for some clothes and run them over to you."

"Okay. Umm, I don't know anything about sizes."

"Don't worry about that. Leave it to me." She hung up. Knowing Felicity, she was probably already on her way out of the door.

I placed the phone on the coffee table and sat back in the chair. My heart went out to Mallory and I felt a profound grief, the likes of which I'd never experienced before.

She never seemed able to catch a break. After her first traumatic experience at the hands of Mister Scary, when she became the

Final Girl at the Bloody Summer Massacre, she became cursed by the Box of Midnight.

Destroying the sorceress's heart within the box was the only way to stop a man named John DuMont from raising an army of the dead. Mallory stabbed the heart with an enchanted blade, even though she knew that doing so would attract a death curse that allowed her only one more year to live.

And now she'd spent three months of that year fighting for survival in Shadow Land. I couldn't even imagine the horror she'd experienced there.

I felt the heavy weight of guilt for most of what had happened to Mallory after the Bloody Summer Massacre. I'd tried to help her track down Mister Scary when the best course of action might have been to let Mallory heal over time without the need for revenge.

If it wasn't for me, she'd never have come into contact with the Box of Midnight and contracted the curse that numbered her days.

And if I hadn't fallen for her and entered into a confusing relationship with her, she might still be living in Dearmont. The confusion between us had eventually driven Mallory to undertake a quest to find Mister

Scary on her own and that had ultimately led her to Shadow Land.

As far as I was concerned, I couldn't do enough to help Mallory because I was the cause of some of her problems.

I closed my eyes and ran over the events of the day in my mind. Other than Mallory getting safely home, the entire day had been a bust. My quest with Merlin had come to a dead end even before it had started and all I'd succeeded in doing was making enemies of two Shadow Watch agents.

I couldn't be sure if Todd and Honoka had come up with the idea of questioning me about my father or if Michael Chester had suggested it to them when he'd requested that I join them on their case. What did I really know about the guy other than the fact that he was my dad's secretary? For all I knew, he could be one of the Cabal infiltrators the Society was trying to weed out.

And speaking of my father, where the hell was he? He'd been gone for weeks now and no one had a clue where he was. Even though he and I didn't exactly get on like best buddies, if he was in trouble or if he had a secret to share, I was sure he'd contact me before anyone else.

We did have a kind of grudging mutual respect.

That said, my respect for him had taken a nosedive after I'd found out that he'd had some sort of magical runes and writing carved onto my bones by witches when I was a child.

That kind of thing can sour a father-son relationship.

I must have fallen asleep in the chair because the next thing I knew, there was a knock on the door. Moving quickly to answer it, I found Felicity on the stoop. She was surrounded by shopping bags.

"Wow," I said. "It looks like you went to town both literally and figuratively."

"Well I wasn't sure of her size," she said, picking up an armful of bags and coming inside. "So I brought a number of things for her to try on. Anything that doesn't fit can be taken back to the store."

I grabbed the rest of the bags and manhandled them into the living room. "There's still a lot of stuff here."

She rolled her eyes jokingly. "It's obvious you're not a woman. You said she needed clothing but there are other things to think about as well. Underwear. Makeup. Shampoo. Beauty products. The list is endless."

I looked at the mountain of bags in the room. "So it seems."

"Is she still asleep?"

"Yeah."

"I don't want to disturb her so I'll just leave these things here and she can try on whatever she wants and I'll return the rest."

"This is really good of you, Felicity. You didn't have to go to this much trouble."

"Nonsense. Mallory is family."

"How are you getting on with the Hawthorne case?"

"We're looking into a car crash that happened on the same night as Jane Hawthorne's Fall party last year."

"Oh? You think that has something to do with Charles saying he saw a car wreck in that smoke?"

"It's possible. It's a slim lead but it's all we have to go on for now so we're following it. How about you? How did you get on with Merlin?"

"It was a total bust. It seems the Shadow Agents who agreed to take me along with them had an ulterior motive; they wanted to question me about my dad."

"Oh, that's a disappointment."

"Yeah, and the guy they were chasing isn't even a Cabal member. He's an occultist who attended a couple of meetings at Lucy Hawthorne's house and thought he was being groomed for greater things. The Watch would have found that out eventually. Probably after they'd tortured the poor guy."

"Oh no, that's horrible."

"Yeah." I shook my head at the thought of what Todd and Honoka might have done to Gerald Garland if they'd had the chance. "Do you ever wonder if we're on the right side?"

"You mean you think we should be working for the Midnight Cabal?"

"No, I don't mean that. I mean do you think we should be working for any organization at all. We have the Society and Cabal at opposite ends of the spectrum, fighting all the time. Meanwhile there are innocent people stuck in the middle who are getting caught up in the war through no fault of their own."

"You long for the good old days," she said. "Before you even knew the Cabal existed."

"I guess so. One of those Watch agents was

trying to humiliate me by suggesting P.I.s just hunt ghosts and deal with the occasional werewolf but actually, that's not humiliating at all. I enjoyed those simple cases. A hint of a mystery and a monster that didn't have political affiliations. Maybe save a life or two. Those were good times."

"Perhaps one day, those times will return."

"Yeah, maybe," I said wistfully.

"I'd best get back to the office and see what else Leon has unearthed about this car wreck a year ago."

"Okay. Is Amy helping you out too?"

"She said she'd drop by after work."

"Cool. I guess I'll see you later then."

"If Mallory wakes up and wants any help trying on the clothes, let me know."

"Okay."

She left the house and closed the door behind her. I watched her get into her Mini and drive away. My relationship with Felicity also ticked the box marked "Confusing." There was something between us that would appear for a brief moment and then disappear again.

Nothing had happened other than a couple of brief kisses that had occurred and then been relegated to the zone of things that were never spoken of. Maybe that was a mistake. Or maybe the kisses had been the mistake and should never have happened in the first place.

Since Felicity and I seemed to have an unspoken agreement not to talk about it, it was difficult to decide one way or the other.

I heard Mallory stirring in bed and went up to see if she was okay.

She was sitting up in bed, comforter clutched to her neck, eyes wide and frightened. When she saw me, she relaxed a little. "Alec, I didn't know where I was for a second. I heard voices."

"You're safe," I said, sitting on the edge of the bed. "You probably heard me talking to Felicity. She went shopping and got some clothes for you."

"That's nice of her. Felicity is a good person."

I nodded. "She is. I'll bring the shopping bags up so you can go through them when you're ready."

"Alec, there's something I have to tell you."

"Sure, what is it?"

"When I left, right after I destroyed the sorceress's heart, I wasn't being totally honest with you."

"Mallory, it doesn't matter why you left. It's in the past."

"It does matter because it isn't in the past; it's affecting me right now. It's something I've had to live with every day since stabbing that heart."

"What is it?"

She took a deep breath and said, "The sorceress is living inside my head."

11

Darkness was falling when Felicity got back to the office. She ascended the stairs from the street to find Leon settled at her desk where she'd left him earlier and Amy sitting in one of the chairs in the small corridor at the top of the stairs, a laptop perched on her knees.

When he saw Felicity, Leon said, "I think we've got something with the car wreck theory. A few things fit into place which may explain the events at the party."

"Sounds interesting," Felicity said, taking a seat next to Amy. "What have we got?"

He came out of the office and stood before them. "Okay, picture the scene. It's a dark and cold October night. Charles Hawthorne should be at his wife's Fall party but instead, he's driving his Rolls Royce Silver Shadow—a classic car, I might add—along a seemingly deserted road that winds through the woods. He's had a few too many and his speed is in excess of the posted speed limit. We're not sure why he's driving when he should be partying but anyway, there he is, tooling along the road in his Rolls."

He held up an eraser in his left hand. "This eraser is Charles." He then held up a pencil in his right hand. "And this pencil is a 1987 Chrysler Town & Country station wagon belonging to the Libby family. It isn't a classic car by any means, in fact it's a beater, but it's served the Libby family well and right now it's transporting Mason Libby, 26, and his brother Owen Libby, 29. We're not exactly sure where they're heading but the important fact is that they are on the same winding road as Charles Hawthorne's silver Rolls.

Leon brought the eraser and pencil together and dropped them both on the floor while he made an "explosion" gesture with his fingers. "What happened when these two cars met on that icy road isn't known for sure but the Libby's car ended up in the woods and

Mason Libby ended up dead. Owen survived but was paralyzed from the waist down."

"That's terrible," Felicity said. She couldn't imagine what it must be like to have your life so horribly changed in an instant like that. "What happened to Charles Hawthorne?"

"Charles Hawthorne hired Jeffery Rose and Seb Powers, two of the best lawyers around, to ensure he wouldn't be implicated in or held responsible for the crash in any way. Rose and Powers did whatever it is that high-powered lawyers do and they got Charles off the hook. The entire thing was swept under the carpet."

Felicity thought about that for a moment. "So if Charles Hawthorne is responsible for the death of Mason Libby, then Owen might be taking revenge."

"He could be," Leon said. "Or it could be the boys' mother Abigail. It makes sense that she or Owen are the ones taking revenge because Owen became wheelchair-bound after the accident and a spell was cast on Charles that put him in the same situation."

"It sounds like someone is taking an eye for an eye," Amy said.

"Do we know how to find Abigail and Owen Libby?" Felicity asked.

Amy nodded. "They live on a farm outside of town."

"Maybe we should talk to them and determine if our theory is correct."

"Sure," Amy said. "We can take my car."

Leon's phone buzzed in his pocket. He took it out and checked it. "I've got a text from Brad Hawthorne. He wants to meet me urgently."

"You should go," Felicity said. "It might be something to do with the case."

"Sure, but in Brad's world an urgent event could be nothing more than the release of a new game."

"You should still meet him just to make sure. Amy and I will visit the Libbys."

"Okay," Leon said, heading down the stairs. "Later."

It was getting late so Felicity turned off the lights in the office and followed Amy downstairs to the street. She locked up and climbed into the passenger seat of the police cruiser. Amy started the engine and they drove through town toward the highway.

Dearmont was getting ready for Halloween. Most of the stores along Main Street had incorporated cobwebs, pumpkins, and skeletons into their window displays and a banner spanning the street announced that the Dearmont Halloween Parade would be held on the 31st.

Even though Felicity dealt with monsters and ghosts as part of her job, she enjoyed the fake versions that made an appearance every Halloween. They were so safe and cute, far from the reality of the real thing.

This was as close as some people would ever get to things that go bump in the night and that was fine with Felicity. Not everyone could handle reality.

Alec had once told her that the thing he liked the least about being a P.I. was the fact that he sometimes had to tell his clients that monsters were real. He believed that ignorance was bliss as far as the paranormal was concerned and although Felicity had disagreed with him at the time, believing that everyone had a right to know the truth about the world they live in, but when she saw the cute ghosts and smiling pumpkins at Halloween, she sometimes wondered if it was better that most people's knowledge of the paranormal extended no further than cute characters that appeared every October.

She wondered how Mallory was doing.

From what Alec had told her, it sounded like the poor girl was in a bad way. Felicity liked Mallory. There had been a time not so long ago when she and Mallory had vied for Alec's attention but Felicity didn't hold that against Mallory. In fact, she chided herself for acting like a silly schoolgirl.

She liked Alec a lot but the more she thought about the times they'd kissed or the times she'd looked at him with longing, the more she realized that she wasn't ready for a relationship with anyone yet.

After all, it was only a few months ago that she'd been considering moving to a cottage in Essex with her fiancé Jason. She couldn't flit from one man to another like that; it just wasn't her.

"What do you think?" Amy asked, pulling Felicity out of her thoughts.

She realized she'd missed part of the conversation. "Sorry," she said. "I was miles away. What did you say?"

"I asked if you thought it might be a good idea to get the Blackwell sisters involved in the search for the Midnight Cabal. It seems to me that they know a lot about what's going on in the magical world. Maybe they can cast a spell or something."

"It's certainly something to keep in mind," Felicity said. They drove out of town and onto the highway. "Amy, can I ask you a question?"

The deputy nodded. "Of course."

"Do you wish you'd never learned that magic and monsters are real?"

Amy seemed to think about the question for a minute before answering. "At first, I was terrified. My entire world was turned upside down. I didn't know what was real anymore. It was like someone had pulled a rug out from under me and revealed an endless abyss beneath my feet."

"That's totally understandable," Felicity said.

"Then I started to just accept it," Amy continued. "I adjusted to my new world view and got on with living my life. But I think I understand why my mom kept me in the dark, even when she knew for a fact that the paranormal was real. She was trying to protect me. I guess the irony is that her death finally opened my eyes to reality.

"It took some time for me to adjust, though. At first, I was so angry that this knowledge had been given to me without me even asking for it. It felt like someone had dumped bag of stinking garbage on my lawn and I had to deal with it."

Felicity nodded. "You've adjusted really well."

"Thanks." She turned into a narrow road that wound through the trees.

Felicity realized this was probably the road where the accident happened. The trees crowded in on both sides of the road and Amy had to slow down for each tight corner. Felicity tried to imagine how treacherous the road would be when it was icy, like it had been a year ago.

"That's the Libby place ahead," Amy said after a couple of minutes. "How are we going to handle this?"

"We should talk to them about the accident," Felicity said.

"They might not want to talk about that if it brings back bad memories."

"In my experience, when people have an axe to grind or they think they're the victims of a miscarriage of justice, they're usually all too willing to talk about it."

"Okay, let's try it."

"I have this as well," Felicity said, showing Amy the crystal shard she was carrying in her pocket. "It glows if it detects magic or magic residue. This should let us know if the surviving Libbys have been taking revenge by magical means."

"Why would they do that?" Amy asked. "It would be easier to shoot Charles Hawthorne wouldn't it?"

"I asked myself the same question when I first learned about the magical attacks. I suppose the answer is that they can only ensure they get the exact result they want if they use magic. For instance, if they want to take Charles's use of his legs away in revenge for what happened to Owen, they might put a bullet in his spine. But that could kill him. Or it might not paralyze him at all. It's too hit or miss. If they use sympathetic magic, though, they can be almost surgical in their precision. A spell will do exactly what you tell it to; a bullet won't."

Amy nodded. "I guess that makes sense."

They arrived at the farmhouse a couple of minutes later. The house sat in darkness. "Looks like no one's home," Amy said. She drove closer and parked the cruiser by the front porch. She killed the engine. "We'll take a look inside."

"Should we do that?" Felicity asked. "Shouldn't we just wait until they get home?"

Amy shook her head and pointed at the door. "The front door's open."

Felicity got out of the car and saw that the front door was ajar and the screen door was hanging precariously from its top hinge.

Amy took a flashlight from her belt and shone the beam over the front of the house and then the door. She stepped up onto the porch and aimed the light down between her boots. "Looks like the porch is covered with dirt."

Felicity joined her and inspected the dark patch on the wooden porch boards. It did indeed look like soil and possibly something else as well. "Is that blood?"

"Could be," Amy said, unholstering her gun. "Try not to step on it. We don't want to compromise any evidence if this is a crime scene."

Felicity knew that what they'd found so far —an open door and some dirt—was hardly the grounds to suspect a crime but she knew why Amy was being so cautious. There was a kind of electricity in the air around the Libby house, something that made the hairs on Felicity's neck and arms rise to attention. She realized her breathing had quickened.

"Perhaps they just went out to the store and left the door open," she said softly, trying to assert some logic to the situation, something that would ease the anxious feeling that bloomed within her.

"The car's over there," Amy said, pointing the flashlight at a brown station wagon parked in the yard.

"Oh," Felicity said. That was that theory out of the window.

Amy pushed the screen door aside. As she did so, the remaining hinge snapped and the metal door crashed onto the porch.

If anyone's in there, Felicity thought, *they know we're here now.* She wished she had some sort of weapon to protect herself.

Amy pushed open the wooden front door with the toe of her boot. She shouted, "This is the Sheriff's Department. Is anyone home?"

The house remained silent.

With her gun and the flashlight gripped in both hands in front of her, Amy entered the building. Felicity followed close behind but made sure she gave the deputy enough room to maneuver should she need it.

They stood in a kitchen. The walls were grimy and there were dishes in the sink but there were no signs of a struggle or a break-in or anything of that nature. The kitchen chairs were neatly arranged around the table and the cabinets were closed.

"More dirt," Felicity whispered to Amy. A dark trail of dirt lay on the linoleum. It led all the way to a small corridor that separated the kitchen from the living room and terminated in a set of stairs that went up to the next floor. The dirt trail didn't lead to either the stairs or the living room, though; it led to an open wooden door in the corridor.

Amy shone her light through the doorway. A set of wooden steps led down to a cellar.

"You smell that?" Amy asked.

For the first time since entering the house, Felicity noticed a smell that reminded her of rotting vegetables. She nodded to Amy. At least this wasn't the sickly-sweet smell of death but in a way, this smelled even worse.

"Stay close," Amy said as she moved through the doorway and down the steps.

Felicity did as ordered. She didn't want to be left alone up here.

They descended to the cellar slowly, the wooden steps creaking under their weight. Amy moved her gun and flashlight in an arc and the light traveled over the cellar's brick walls. It came to rest on a workbench that had been set up in one corner.

"There's something on it," Amy said, moving forward. She stopped suddenly and held out a hand to stop Felicity. "Be careful, there's a hole in the floor." Aiming the flashlight down, she revealed a crude oblong hole in the dirt floor. Felicity guessed the hole's dimensions to be approximately three feet wide and eight feet long. It looked to be around six feet deep. The standard size of a grave.

A pile of dirt and a shovel lay next to the hole. The grave had either been dug recently and was awaiting an occupant or something had recently been unearthed from it.

Stepping carefully around the hole, Felicity joined Amy at the workbench. Amy had something in her hand. She gave it to Felicity. "Can you read this?"

Felicity took the slim leather-bound book from Amy and read the title stamped on the cover. *Et Conjuratio de Nocte Sanguine.* She leafed through a few of the pages. Like the title, the text was in Latin with diagrams of magical symbols.

"What does it say?" Amy asked.

"It's a Latin translation of an older work, a resurrection spell. She showed Amy the title on the cover. "The Conjuration of the Midnight Blood."

Amy looked from the book to the open grave. "Are you thinking what I'm thinking?"

"That the spell was used to bring Mason Libby back from the dead? Yes."

They left the cellar. Felicity took the book with her because she wanted to study it in detail later when she got home. When they got to the first floor, Amy used her light to track the trail of dirt across the kitchen floor and out of the door. "Where did they go?"

"Maybe they went to the Hawthorne residence to commit their final act of revenge?"

"Then why is the car still here? The Hawthorne house is miles away."

They went outside and Amy shone the light around the general area. As well as the house, there was a barn and a toolshed. Both seemed deserted.

"We should check around back," Amy said.

Felicity followed her around the side of the house. She still felt a charge of nervous energy running through her veins, even more so now that she suspected black magic had been performed here recently. Although checking the crystal shard was almost redundant at this point, she took it out of her pocket and held it on her palm. It shone brighter than Amy's flashlight.

A chill wind had begun to blow through the trees, rustling the leaves so that they sounded as if they were whispering. Felicity put the crystal back into her pocket and shivered.

They reached the backyard and Amy suddenly shouted, "There!" She increased her pace, almost running toward a bulky object on the ground. Felicity ran after her and when Amy finally stopped, could see what had alarmed the deputy.

A wheelchair lay on the ground on its side. A young man Felicity assumed to be Owen Libby was sprawled on the grass. It was obvious that he was dead. The grass around his body was stained with blood that looked black in the weak moonlight and a huge gash had been torn from Owen's neck to his navel. He wore wire-rimmed glasses but one lens was shattered and the eye behind it was nothing more than a bloody mess.

Felicity felt sick. She turned away from the grisly scene and swallowed back acidic bile that rose in her throat. This young man had clearly been murdered and it looked like his chest cavity had been ripped open and parts of his body had been removed.

"Come on," Amy said, putting a gentle hand on Felicity's shoulder. "I'm going to call this in."

Felicity followed her back to the car, her mind racing. She knew that black magic spells usually demanded a sacrifice and resurrection was one of the blackest forms of all magic. Had the Conjuration of the Midnight Blood demanded a terrible sacrifice?

Before they left the yard, she looked back at the bulky shape lying beneath the pale moonlight. She hardly dared contemplate what she knew had probably happened here.

Had a mother sacrificed one of her sons so that another might be brought back from the dead?

12

I brought the two mugs of coffee into the living room and gave one to Mallory. She was sitting in the easy chair with her legs curled up.

While I was waiting for the coffee maker to do its thing, she'd gotten dressed and now wore a pair of jeans and a cream-colored sweater.

I sat on the sofa and waited for her to tell the story in her own time.

Mallory took a sip of the coffee and grimaced. "I haven't tasted this in a while."

"Would you like something else? I have tea."

"No, I might as well get used to things again." She swallowed some more of the coffee before continuing. "The moment I plunged the dagger into the heart of the sorceress, something entered my body. I felt...different. At first, I thought it was the curse, that I could somehow sense it inside of me but after a while, I began to see a woman in my peripheral vision. Like, I'd see her in the corner of the room but when I turned to look, she wasn't there. I began to believe I was going crazy."

"You could have told me. Maybe I could have helped."

She shook her head. "I needed to be alone, think things through. The curse made me realize it was probably now or never where hunting Mister Scary was concerned and seeing the imaginary woman reinforced that belief. If I was losing my mind, I had to act quickly before the madness overtook me completely."

I nodded and tried to imagine the mental torment Mallory must have been going through.

"I spent some time traveling down the east coast, staying in one cheap hotel after another, waiting for some clue to appear and give me a direction," she said. "Every night, I had vivid dreams of an ancient city and I saw scenes of life in the palace there. I saw the Pharaoh, Amenhotep, and the high priest Rekhmire. I saw all of this through the eyes of Tia, the sorceress who cast spells and enchantments for the pharaoh. I also saw the moment Rekhmire murdered her and cut out her heart."

She'd been gazing at the table while telling this part of her story. Now, she looked at me with tears in her eyes. "I felt everything she'd felt, Alec. These weren't just dreams; they were her memories and I was sharing in them. I knew then that I wasn't crazy; the sorceress was inside my head. When I stabbed her heart, Rekhmire's death curse wasn't the only thing that became attached to me. So did Tia. Now, I sometimes see her when I look into a mirror. Instead of my reflection staring back at me, it's her."

"I can't imagine what that must be like," I said.

"It isn't too bad. At first, I fought the sorceress and the visions—tried to get them out of my head—but now I accept them. Tia is a lot like me; I want revenge on Mister Scary and she wants revenge on Rekhmire."

This kind of reminded me of Merlin possessing Sheriff Cantrell but at least in this instance, Mallory was still in control of her own body, and her mind wasn't locked away in some magical prison.

"When I was in Shadow Land," she said, "I became thankful that Tia was with me. Her being there meant I wasn't completely alone. She helped me get through some dark times."

My phone rang and Leon's name appeared on the screen. "Sorry," I said to Mallory. "I have to get this."

She nodded. "Yes, of course."

"Leon," I said, answering the call. "What's up?"

"Hey, man, we have a problem. Brad Hawthorne texted me a little while ago. He wanted to meet me at his sister's house in Rockport, said it was urgent. When I got here, the door was open so I came inside. There's something you need to see. I'm sending you a photo."

The phone buzzed and I navigated to the text Leon had sent. He'd taken a picture of Lucy's living room, where I'd sat and talked to Lucy earlier that day. But now everything in the room was out of order. The coffee table with the carved tentacle legs lay on its side, surrounded by hundreds of paperback books, which had been pulled from the shelves. Lucy's computer had been overturned. Papers and notebooks lay on the floor.

"There's no sign of Lucy or her brother?" I asked Leon.

"I checked everywhere. There's no one here."

"Okay, listen, I'll finish talking with Mallory while you drive back from Rockport and I'll meet you at the office in an hour."

"Mallory's back?"

"Yeah, she is. Bring something of Lucy's from the house. Something personal. Maybe one of her notebooks or a pen or something. We can get the Blackwell sisters to cast a locator spell and find out where she and Brad are."

"You got it. On my way." He ended the call.

"Trouble?" Mallory asked.

"Yeah, someone connected to a case we're working has gone missing. I'm going to have to go to the office and—" I cut off my own words when I heard something small crash through the window. It landed on the floor between us.

"What the hell's that?" Mallory was out of her chair, standing by the coffee table and looking down at the object on the carpet.

It was ball—no larger than a baseball—

made of a dull metal and inscribed with runes. I had no idea what it was but since someone had thrown it into the house, I knew it wasn't good.

"We need to get out of here!" I said to Mallory.

But as soon as I got the words out, a blinding flash of light exploded from the ball.

Then everything went black.

13

As they left the Libby farm behind, Felicity ran over the scene they'd just witnessed in her head. It didn't make sense that Abigail Libby would sacrifice one of her sons to bring back the other. What mother would do that?

It began to rain and Amy turned on the wipers. Felicity listened to the repetitive *whirr* as they arced across the windshield every few seconds.

Amy hit the brakes suddenly and the cruiser skidded to a halt.

"What are you doing?" Felicity asked.

"That woman we just passed back there," Amy said, killing the siren. "That was Abigail Libby."

Felicity turned in her seat to look out of the

car's rear window. She could barely make out the silhouette of someone walking along the edge of the highway.

Amy got out of the car and sprinted back along the highway toward the silhouette. Felicity took off her seatbelt and got out as well, squinting against the headlights of the oncoming traffic. As she followed Amy, she saw the silhouetted woman—the person Amy had said was Abigail Libby—stumble and fall.

Amy tried to get the woman to her feet and Felicity rushed over to help.

"Help me get her into the car," Amy said.

They each took an arm and guided Abigail into the backseat of the cruiser.

Amy turned on the interior light. In its dim glow, Felicity could see that Abigail was in her fifties with gray hair scraped back into a ponytail. She was a thin woman with sunken eyes and a sallow complexion. Felicity could smell alcohol on her breath. Her head lolled to one side and she mumbled something incoherent.

"Abigail," Amy said. "What are you doing wandering along the highway?"

Dressed in nothing more than jeans and a

black T-shirt, Abigail was hardly dressed for the weather.

"I'm just going for a walk," Abigail said.

"Along the highway at night?"

Abigail looked around at her surroundings with bleary eyes. "Is that where I am?"

"Did you walk here from your house?"

She shook her head. "I can't go to the house. Owen says I'm not allowed. So I stay away."

"What do you mean? Why aren't you allowed to go to your own house?"

Abigail shrugged exaggeratedly. "I don't know. Owen said it would spoil the surprise. He's a good boy. Both of my boys are good boys. Look, I have a photo of them." She patted the pockets of her jeans as if looking for something but couldn't find it. "I don't know where it is."

"Abigail, what are—"

"Do you know it's a year and a day ago that my Mason was taken from me? That's a long time to be without my son."

"I know," Amy said. "I'm sorry for your loss."

Abigail squinted at Amy. "Are you the police? Am I in trouble?"

"I am the police and I'm not sure if you're in

trouble or not. What can you tell me about your son Owen?"

"He's a good boy. He's going to surprise me, he said. A big surprise. That's nice, don't you think?"

Amy nodded. "Uh huh. Do you know that the surprise was?"

Abigail let out a short laugh. "No, because then it wouldn't be a surprise."

"When's the last time you saw Owen?" Amy asked.

She frowned, obviously trying to remember. "A couple days ago I think. He told me I had to stay at a motel and I couldn't go home until he said it was okay."

Amy looked at Felicity with sadness in her eyes. Felicity was sure the same expression was showing on her own face. Abigail didn't seem to know that Owen was dead.

"That's the last time I saw Owen," Abigail said. "Was when he said I had to stay at a motel and that there'd be a surprise waiting for me when I got home. The last time I saw my other son, Mason, was more than a year ago. Isn't that sad? I have a picture somewhere." She patted her pockets again. "It's in one of my pockets but I don't know which one."

"So what are you doing out here in the rain?" Amy asked.

"I got bored in the motel room," she said. "Or maybe I was sad. I'm not sure. So I came outside and went for a walk."

"Were you heading anywhere in particular?"

Abigail frowned as if deep in thought and then said, "Yes. Yes, I was."

"Where were you going?"

"To the cemetery. To Mason's grave."

"Why were you going there?"

"Because the last time I went there with Owen, he said to me, "Mom, this is the last time you'll ever have to come here." Well that isn't right, is it? Why wouldn't I visit my son's grave ever again? So I'm going to walk there tonight to prove Owen wrong." She laughed. "That'll show him."

"I have a better idea," Amy said. "Why don't we take you somewhere safe and warm and dry?"

"Is there a minibar?"

"No, there isn't a minibar but there is coffee."

"Okay, sounds good."

Felicity and Amy got into the front seats. Leaving the lights flashing, Amy joined the traffic on the highway. "I'm going to have to take her to the station."

"We should warn Charles Hawthorne first," Felicity said. "His house is quite secure but he needs to know that Mason Libby might be on his way there."

"The question is," Amy said, lowering her voice. "If Abigail wasn't involved in raising Mason from the dead—and it appears she wasn't—then who was?"

"Owen definitely had a hand in it," Felicity said. "Those things he said to his mother about not having to visit the grave anymore and telling her he had a big surprise for her suggest he was planning to resurrect Mason."

Amy nodded. "Yeah, but he didn't kill himself. Someone sacrificed him. So somebody was working with him and then betrayed him."

"That's what it looks like," Felicity said.

They reached the driveway that led to the mansion. The security guard came out of his booth as soon as he saw them approach.

Amy rolled down her window and shouted at him, "Let us in. Police business."

This wasn't strictly true, of course; the police had no idea that the body in the Libby's yard and the empty grave in the cellar were in any way connected to Charles Hawthorne and might mean he was in danger but the lie was necessary because otherwise, Hawthorne would probably refuse to let them onto his property.

The guard didn't offer a word of protest. He went back into the booth and the gate swung open. Amy drove onto the gravel parking area and switched off the lights and the engine.

"We'll be back in a couple of minutes," she said to Abigail.

There was no reply. Felicity glanced into the backseat and saw that Abigail was sleeping soundly.

Before they had a chance to get out of the car, the front door opened and the butler came outside with a worried look on his face. "Is there a problem?"

"Is Mr Hawthorne at home?" Amy asked.

"Yes, of course."

"We need to speak with him."

"All right." He led them into the foyer. "I'll make Mr Hawthorne aware of your presence. Can I give him any details of what this visit is in relation to?"

"No, we'll tell him everything to his face."

"Very well." He disappeared through a door

and returned moments later with Charles Hawthorne.

"What is it?" Hawthorne said, looking them over.

"Mr Hawthorne, we've come to warn you that you may be in danger," Felicity said.

"I know I'm in danger. That's why I hired your boss to find out who I'm in danger from."

"We believe it's Mason Libby."

Hawthorne looked bemused. "What are you talking about? Mason Libby is dead."

"Yes, he is," Amy said. "But that doesn't mean he isn't coming here right now to take revenge for his death."

Hawthorne looked worried but acted as if confused. "What do you mean?"

"We know you caused the accident that killed Mason," Amy told him.

"No, that isn't true. The matter went to court and I was completely exonerated."

"I'm not talking about technicalities or whatever your lawyers told the court," Amy said. "I'm talking about the reality of the situation. And the reality is that he might be on his way here."

He narrowed his eyes. Felicity couldn't work out if he believed their theory or not.

"Would you like me to stay here?" Felicity asked.

"No, I wouldn't. We have security guards, walls, and cameras. What the hell could you do?"

"The nature if what we're dealing with—"

"Where's Harbinger?" he asked, cutting her off. "Why isn't he here?"

"He's busy with something else at the moment."

"That isn't good enough. When I hire someone, I expect the head man to be working for me, not his assistant. Get out of my house, both of you."

"Mr Hawthorne," Amy protested.

He sighed. "Wesley, please escort our guests out of the house. Get security to help you if need be."

"Never mind," Amy said. "We're leaving." She and Felicity went out into the rain and hurried to the cruiser.

When they got inside the vehicle and closed the doors, Abigail stirred in the backseat. "Huh? What's that?"

"Everything's okay, Abigail," Amy said. "Go back to sleep."

Abigail peered through the windshield at

the Hawthorne mansion. "Hey, this is the place. This is where Mason and Owen were going on the night they had the accident. I have a photo somewhere." She patted her pockets and this time came up with something. She held it up so Amy and Felicity could see it.

"Don't they look sweet?" she asked proudly.

Felicity looked at the crumpled photograph. It showed Owen and Mason standing on the porch of the Libby farmhouse, arms around each other. They were smiling at the camera and wearing tuxedos.

"They look lovely," she told Abigail.

But when Amy started the car and they drove away from the mansion, Felicity was wondering how coincidental it was that Owen and Mason crashed into Charles Hawthorne's Rolls Royce miles away from here on a night when all three of them were supposed to be attending the same party.

14

When I came to, it wasn't a slow rise from the depths of unconsciousness. There was no gradual awareness of my surroundings. I was awake suddenly, my eyes snapping open to instantly look for a way out of my predicament.

I was chained to a chair. Sitting across from me, Mallory was also restrained but with ropes instead of chains. Her eyes were closed and her head lolled to one side. She was still out.

I looked around, taking in my surroundings. The room was windowless and the walls were painted with sigils and patterns. I recognized some of them as wards and others as magic-nullifying symbols.

A single bare bulb hung from the ceiling,

casting a circle of pale yellow light upon Mallory and me.

There was one door, which was painted with magical glyphs in the same manner as the walls.

Mallory woke up suddenly, her eyes wide as they looked first at me and then at our prison.

"Where are we?" she whispered.

"Some sort of room that's been designed to hold paranormal creatures or people with magical abilities," I said.

"What's that around your neck?"

With the weight of the chains on my shoulders, arms, and legs, I hadn't noticed anything in particular around my neck. "What does it look like?"

"A collar with magical symbols etched into it."

"Oh crap."

"What is it? What's wrong?"

"We're in the hands of the Shadow Watch, probably the two bozos Merlin cast a spell on."

"Is that bad?"

"It could be. They seem to think I know where my father is. This collar around my neck forces me to tell the truth."

The door opened. Todd Benson and

Honoka Chan walked into the room, still dressed like extras from a Matrix movie.

"Harbinger," Todd said, circling us slowly, walking just beyond the circle of light, "Who'd have thought you'd end up here?"

"Not me," I said. "There's been a misunderstanding."

He grinned. "That's right. You misunderstood why we agreed to let you ride with us. Did you really think we'd give information about the Midnight Cabal to a lowly P.I. like you?"

I shrugged. "I guess I thought you were decent people. That we were all on the same team."

"If we're all on the same team, Harbinger, then why have you been keeping secrets from us? Hmm?"

"Secrets?"

He leaned in close to my face, his eyes boring into mine. "You know what I'm talking about. Are you keeping secrets from us, Harbinger?"

I tried to say, "No" but the word that came out of my mouth was, "Yes." Damned collar.

"Aha!" he said, grinning. "Now we're getting somewhere."

My mind began to race. The truth was, I had no idea where my father was but I did have another secret, one so powerful that I'd once asked a *satori* to erase it from my head. I knew where the Spear of Destiny was hidden. That wasn't the kind of information I wanted to give to anyone, especially not the super-tool known as Todd Benson.

He was going to question me regarding my father but could inadvertently reveal something extremely dangerous.

My one saving grace was how the collar worked. It made me answer direct questions with a truthful "yes" or "no" but that was all. It didn't compel the wearer to answer open-ended questions.

For instance, Todd could ask me if I had a secret and I would be forced to answer "yes" or "no," whichever was the truth. But if he asked me, "What secrets are you hiding, Harbinger?" the collar wouldn't make me reply, "I know where the Spear of Destiny is hidden."

It was like playing Twenty Questions except for the fact that the interrogator could ask as many "yes" or "no" questions as he or she liked.

If Todd was an experienced interrogator, he might be able to get to the truth simply by asking me enough "yes" or "no" questions. I couldn't let that happen.

He began by asking the question that was the crux of the matter. "Do you know where your father is?"

"No," I said.

He seemed a little shaken by that. He'd probably been sure I'd answer in the affirmative.

"Okay," he said, nodding to himself. "Okay. Let's try something else. Has your father ever given you something and asked you to hide it for him?"

"No."

He pursed his lips and seemed to dwell on that answer. "Okay, fine. Maybe you didn't hide it for him. Or maybe he didn't *ask* you to. Have you ever hidden something for your father?"

"No."

His frustration was almost palpable. It seemed to hang in the air between us like a heavy boulder ready to drop. Todd shot a look at Honoka, who was standing by the door. She shrugged at him helplessly.

"Okay, here's one I asked you before, only you weren't wearing a collar then. Let's see what you say now. Have you ever heard of the Melandra Codex?"

"Yes."

His face brightened. "I knew it!" Pacing the floor excitedly, he tried to work out his next question.

"Wait a minute," Honoka said from the shadows by the door. "Harbinger, had you ever heard of the Melandra Codex before Todd mentioned it to you earlier today?"

"No."

"Fuck!" Todd slammed his fist into the palm of his hand.

"I don't think he knows anything," Honoka told him.

"He does. He knows something. He said he has a secret."

"Everyone has secrets, Todd," I said.

He pointed at me accusingly and shook his head. "No, Harbinger, you're not getting out of it that easily. You know something big. Okay, you may not know it's called the Melandra Codex. So I'll ask you this: do you know the location of something your father has hidden from the Society of Shadows?"

"No."

Todd didn't say anything but a vein in his forehead began to pulse.

"You should let me go now," I said.

"No, you're not going anywhere. Do you know where a powerful item is hidden?"

I tried to stop myself from saying anything but the word just slid past my lips. "Yes."

"Has this item been hidden because it's very powerful?"

"Yes."

"See," he said to Honoka. "Now we're getting somewhere."

She sighed. "He doesn't know anything about his father or the Codex. That's all we were told to find out. Whatever you're doing now isn't part of our job."

"Of course it's part of our job. We can't let pissant P.I.s like him make us look stupid."

"You don't need me to do that," I told him. "You're doing a fine job all by yourself."

He gestured to me and said to Honoka, "See? He's got a smart mouth. For all we know, he's a Cabal sympathizer."

She shook her head at Todd. "It's easy to find out." Directing her attention at me, she asked, "Are you a Cabal sympathizer?"

"No."

"Let him go," she said to Todd.

"Not until I find out what he's hiding."

Mallory spoke to the Shadow Watch agent for the first time. Her words were tense, almost whispered through gritted teeth. "You really need to let us go right now."

Todd looked at her and grinned. "Is that so? You know there's a reason you're only bound with ropes instead of chains, right? Harbinger may be nothing more than a two-bit ghost chaser but I have to be a tiny bit careful of him because I've heard some stories. But you're nothing. The amount of threat you pose to me is less than zero so don't sit there telling me what I need to do."

"You don't know who I am." Her head had dropped forward, her hair falling over her face.

"Mallory Bronson," Todd said, pacing slowly around the room. "Only survivor of the Bloody Summer Massacre. So-called Final Girl. Location unknown for the past couple of months because you've been chasing the guy who murdered your friends all those years ago. I guess when you find the guy, you're gonna call on your ghost hunter friend here to help you take revenge. Is that right?"

She didn't answer him. Mallory had become silent.

"Am I right?" Todd pressed.

"Todd, leave her alone," Honoka said. "She's nobody. I don't even know why you insisted we bring her here."

"Because she's a friend of his." Todd pointed at me. "And that means she might know something about the Codex." He leaned forward, getting in my face. "Did you tell your friend, Mallory Bronson, where the Melandra Codex is?"

"Todd, we've already established he doesn't know anything about the Codex." From the tone in her voice, it was clear she was losing her patience with him. "Let's finish up here. We'll wipe their minds and call it a day."

I looked at her. "Wipe our minds?"

"Don't worry, you'll only forget about this meeting. The spell we use is very precise and hardly ever goes wrong."

"It never goes wrong," Todd said.

"There was that one time in Baltimore."

He nodded. "Oh, yeah. It hardly ever goes wrong." Standing back, he looked at me with narrowed eyes. "But before we do the spell, I still want to know what this guy is hiding.

Hell, if the spell goes wrong like it did in Baltimore, a powerful artifact might be lost forever."

Honoka shook her head. "No, Todd."

"Is the powerful artifact hidden in this country?" he asked me.

"No."

He raised an eyebrow. "Is it in Europe?"

"Yes." Damn it. This line of questioning had to stop right now.

"Eastern Europe?"

"No."

"Northern Europe?"

"No."

"Western Europe?"

"Yes."

"Germany?"

"No."

"Austria?"

"No."

"Todd, this isn't right," Honoka said. "This isn't what we were asked to do."

"France?"

"Yes."

"Aha! France!" He leaned in closer to me. "What is this item? Is it a weapon?"

"Yes."

Rubbing his hands together, he said, "This is getting even more interesting. Is it a sword?"

"No."

"Dagger?"

"No."

"Todd, stop this right now," Honoka shouted at him.

"Shut up!" He pushed away from my chair and jabbed his finger at her. "I have every right to do this. If we suspect the enemy is hiding something from us, we have the right to find out what it is."

"Just stop for one second and listen to yourself," she said. "He isn't some high-ranking Cabal member we've brought in for questioning; he's a P.I. We all work for the same organization. He isn't the enemy."

Mallory, whose head was still lolling forward, her hair hanging over her face, said in a strained voice, "He isn't the enemy you need to worry about. I am." She whipped her head up and I saw that her face was covered with hieroglyphs. They seemed to be under her skin, as if the symbols were part of her skull and her skin was stretched over them.

Her eyes had also changed. The usually-hazel-colored irises were as black as midnight.

Mallory whispered something in a language I didn't understand and the ropes that bound her unwound and slithered across the floor like snakes.

Pure panic had entered Todd's eyes. "What the fuck? Why aren't the wards working? Why aren't the wards working?" He stepped back, trying to get as far away from Mallory as he could but she flicked her wrist and he was sent crashing into the wall.

Honoka was reaching for something inside her coat but whatever it was, I doubt her fingers even made contact with it before she too was flung against the wall.

Mallory touched the chains that bound me to the chair. They slithered to the floor and I got up, trying to shake the creepy feeling of having steel snakes sliding over my body.

"Mallory," I said, "What's happened to you?"

"Not Mallory," she said. Her voice was cracked and strained, as if it were trying to reach her mouth from somewhere deep inside her. "Tia."

"Tia," I said. "We have to get out of here." I removed the bolt that held the collar in place around and my neck and took it off.

Tia indicated Todd and Honoka, both of

whom were climbing to their feet. "First these two must die."

"No," I told her. "We're not going to do that."

"They are your enemies."

"We're not going to kill them."

She looked at the two Shadow Agents and I got the feeling she was contemplating whether or not to kill them anyway. Then she pointed at the animated chains and traced her finger through the air toward Todd. He tried to run for the door but the chains were too fast for him. They slithered over his body and tightened like boa constrictors. He fell to the floor, arms bound behind his back, and was knocked out cold when his head hit the concrete.

Tia performed the same action with the ropes. They slithered toward Honoka, who raised her hands in surrender and then sat in the corner, putting her wrists together in front of her as the ropes wound around her.

"I'm sorry this had to happen, Harbinger," Honoka said. "Todd is just...he gets a little crazy sometimes."

"I don't want to see you or him ever again," I told her. "You've confirmed that I don't know anything about my father's whereabouts or whatever damned Codex you're looking for. Leave me alone or it won't end so nicely next time."

She gave me a nod of understanding. "We did the job we were sent to do, which was to ascertain if you knew anything about your father or the Melandra Codex. You don't. You won't be hearing from us again."

"Just tell me one thing," I said. "What the hell is the Melandra Codex?"

She shrugged against the ropes. "I have no idea. I wish I'd never heard of the damned thing."

I couldn't argue with that. Whatever the Melandra Codex was, it had already caused enough trouble that I also wished I'd never heard of it.

"Where are we?" I asked Honoka. "Where is this room located?"

"We're in a house in Bangor. It's a Shadow Watch safe house."

"Is there anyone else here at the moment?"

She shook her head.

"We're going to take your vehicle so we can get home. Where are the keys?"

She sighed. "In the kitchen."

I opened the door and discovered we were in the basement of the house. A set of wooden steps led up to the first floor. We ascended them and I found the keys for the SUV on the kitchen table.

Leading Tia outside into the rain, I found the vehicle parked on the street and climbed in behind the wheel. She got into the passenger seat and gazed out of the water-streaked windshield for a moment before her head lolled forward again and her eyes closed.

Hoping Mallory was going to come back, I started the engine and checked the gas. The tank was almost full. I wasn't exactly sure where in Bangor we were so I fired up the GPS and punched in the address of my office. According to the onboard computer, we'd arrive there in less than an hour.

Mallory lifted her head and I was pleased to see her hazel eyes. The hieroglyphs were gone.

"Do you remember what happened?" I asked her.

She nodded. "I'm totally aware of what's going on when Tia takes over. It isn't like she suppresses me or anything, more like we work together. It's symbiotic."

"Okay." I didn't like the idea of Mallory

being possessed by Tia any more than I liked the idea of Sheriff Cantrell being possessed by Merlin. Symbiotic or not, Tia didn't belong in Mallory's body any more than Merlin belonged in Cantrell's. There was nothing I could do about it at the moment, though.

Right now, we needed to get home.

Mallory looked at the time on the dashboard display. "We've been gone for almost two hours."

"Yeah, that magic grenade really did a number on us. They managed to drive us all the way here without us knowing anything about it."

"I was referring to the fact that you told Leon you'd meet him at your office an hour ago."

"Damn it. I need to find a phone." I presumed my cell was still sitting on the coffee table at home.

I needed to contact Leon because when I hadn't turned up at the office, he'd probably gone ahead and tried to locate Brad and Lucy Hawthorne on his own.

15

Standing in the doorway of the Harbinger P.I. building, trying to stay out of the rain, Leon checked his watch again. It was only two minutes since he'd last checked it. Alec was exactly forty-two minutes late.

He checked his phone. No reply to the six calls he'd made or the eight texts he'd sent. He wondered if he should drive to Alec's and see what the hell was going on or go ahead with the plan to take an item of Lucy's to the Blackwell sisters.

He also wondered if he should be worried that Alec hadn't shown but reminded himself that Alec had said on the phone that Mallory was back. There was some kind of relationship going on between those two that was hard to miss. Whatever the reason for Alec's absence, Leon was sure it was something to do with that.

"I'm not getting in the way of anyone's love life," he said, grinning. He'd just have to visit the Blackwell sisters in his own. By the time Alec finally returned those calls, he might have already found and rescued Brad and Lucy single-handedly.

Well, maybe not single-handedly. Leon was pragmatic enough to realize that he might need help so he called Michael, his butler.

Michael answered immediately. "Yes, sir?"

"Michael, we're going on a hunt for two missing siblings. Bring the RV and the weapons and meet me at Blackwell Books."

"Very good, sir."

Leon hung up and put the phone into the pocket of his jeans. He rushed through the rain to the Testarossa and slid inside. The engine purred into life when he started it and then settled into a throaty purr. Leon drove along Main Street toward Blackwell Books. The bookstore was only a few hundred yards from the Harbinger P.I. office but Leon saw no reason to get wet unnecessarily. The bookstore's lights were on, which meant the

Blackwell sisters were probably in there. He cut the engine, climbed out of the car, and hurried through the door of Blackwell Books.

As he entered the store, a bell above the door rang and Victoria Blackwell appeared from the stacks. As usual, she wore a black lace dress that reached to her ankles, Her long, dark hair was arranged neatly on top of her head.

"Leon, what a surprise!" She drifted toward him and took his hands. "You're here for a spell, aren't you?" Closing her eyes while still keeping hold of his hands, she added, "A locator spell. Is someone missing, dear?"

"Yeah," he said. "The owner of this notebook." He showed her the pocket-sized notebook he'd picked up at Lucy's house.

She took it from him and examined it closely. "Yes, this will do nicely. Come on through to the back room. Devon will be pleased to see you. It's been too long!"

He followed her through the maze of bookshelves to a closed door at the back of the shop. Victoria opened it and led him into a small room where her sister Devon sat at a table poring over a huge book that looked hundreds of years old. Leon could see that the writing in the book was a swirling script that had been written directly onto the pages, not printed there by a press.

Devon looked up and smiled when she saw Leon. "Leon, what brings you to our door?"

"A locator spell," Victoria said.

"Oh, is someone missing? It isn't Alec, is it?"

"No, I have a good idea where he is," Leon said. "This notebook belongs to a woman named Lucy Hawthorne. She and her brother have vanished and there's good reason to suspect they were taken against their will."

"Oh dear," Devon said. "Do you have anything belonging to Brad?'

"No, but I think they're together. So if we find Lucy, we also find her brother."

"All right, we'll give it a shot," Victoria said. She went to a shelf and began rummaging for something while Devon closed the book she'd been reading and removed it from the table.

Victoria found what she'd been looking for and unrolled a map of Maine on the table.

"We assume they're still in the state do we?" she asked Leon.

He shrugged. "I don't know. It's probably a good place to start."

Victoria placed Lucy's notebook next to the

map. Devon returned with a small brass dish, which she also placed close to the map.

"Now we're going to have to use a small part of the notebook," Victoria said. "Perhaps a page from the back. I'm sure Lucy Hawthorne won't mind since we're using it to find out where she is." She ripped a corner from one of the pages in the book and placed it into the brass dish. Devon took a matchbook from a pocket somewhere in her dress and lit one before touching the flame to the paper.

When the paper was reduced to ash, Victoria pinched some between her fingers and thumb and recited a few words before crumbling the ash over the map while moving her hand in a circle.

Instead of falling straight down onto the map, the ash seemed to have a life of its own. Each speck twisted and floated to the same location on the map, forming a small circle there.

"Oh, that isn't good," Victoria said, looking down at the circle of ash.

"What is it?" Leon asked.

"They seem to be on a boat." She pointed at the ash. It had fallen onto the rightmost edge of the map away from land.

"Let me try a different map," Victoria said, going to the shelf again and then returning with a map that showed the east coast and a large stretch of the Atlantic Ocean.

She repeated the spell. The ash formed a circle in the ocean east of Long Island and south of Nantucket.

"They're definitely on a boat," Victoria said.

"Can you get me there?" Leon asked. "The same way you sent me and Alec to England?"

Victoria looked uncertainly at the circle of ash on the map. "I'm not sure. A moving target like that could be very difficult to hit. If anything went wrong, you'd end up in the sea miles from land."

"Unfortunately, we can't use the spell anyway," Devon said. "The destination has to be a church, stone circle, burial ground, or something like that."

"Oh yes, of course," Victoria said. "There won't be anything like that on a boat."

Leon felt helpless. He knew exactly where Lucy and Brad were but had no way to get there.

"Wait a minute," Devon said, "I have an idea. It's a long shot but it might work." She went to the shelf, which Leon now realized contained dozens of maps and looked through them until she found one that showed a close up of the area on which the ash had landed on the larger scale map.

Devon ripped some more paper from Lucy's notebook and cast the locator spell. Once she had a location pinpointed, she went to a desk in the corner of the room and switched on a computer there. After looking something up online, she returned to the map and used a ruler, which she'd taken from one of the desk drawers, to calculate the longitude and latitude of the ash circle.

Once she'd worked that out, she cast the locator spell again. The new circle of ash landed slightly south of the original.

Devon nodded to herself and stared at the map, obviously deep in thought. Then she used the rulers to locate a precise area of the sea where she used a marker to draw a tiny "X."

"What have you discovered?" Victoria asked.

"The boat is moving south along the coast," Devon said. "If it continues on its present heading, it will cross over this "X" I've marked on the map. Once it passes over the "X," we have a tiny window during which we can get Leon on board."

Victoria frowned at her sister. "I must admit I'm confused, dear sister. How can the spell possibly work?"

Leon was thinking the same thing. He wanted to find Lucy and Brad but he didn't want to drown in the Atlantic.

A bell sounded in the shop and Devon looked at Leon. "Are you expecting your friend Michael?"

"Yeah, I told him to meet me here."

"Well he's here. I'll go and greet him. I assume he'll be accompanying you on this adventure?"

Leon nodded.

Devon went out through the door and reappeared moments later with Leon's butler. Michael was dressed in a black sweater and jeans and wore a black wool watch cap. He looked more like a cat burglar than a butler.

"I brought the RV and the weapons, sir," he said when he saw Leon.

"Great," Leon said. "It looks like the RV will be redundant, though. The Blackwells are going to use a spell to get us onto a boat in the

Atlantic where we're going to carry out a rescue operation."

"Very good, sir," Michael said, totally unfazed by what he'd just been told. "May I ask who we're rescuing?"

"Lucy and Brad Hawthorne have been kidnapped."

Michael nodded. "Do we know by whom, sir?"

"No, we'll find that out when we get there." Leon turned to Devon. "You were going to explain how the spell will work."

"It's quite simple, really," she said, pointing at the "X" on the map. "This is the location of the wreck of an Italian liner called the *Andrea Doria*. She sank in 1956 with forty-six casualties. It's a burial ground."

Victoria's face lit up. "Yes, that'll do!"

"There's a slight drawback," Devon said. "We can only bring you back while the boat is in the area of the wreck. You have to find Brad and Lucy in that short window if you want the spell to bring you all back here."

"We'll find a way to make it work," Leon said. "Maybe we can stop the boat and drop the anchor or something."

Devon cast the locator spell again and checked the coordinates of the latest circle of ash. "The boat will be sailing over the wreck in seven minutes and we need time to prepare the spell."

"Let's do it," Leon said.

"I'll get the weapons, sir." Michael left the room. He came back a minute later carrying a black canvas bag. Inside was a selection of guns and bladed weapons.

Leon chose a Mossberg mag-fed shotgun and a Glock 30 handgun. He also took a folding tactical knife, which he placed into his pocket.

"What about you, Michael?" he asked the butler. "What are you taking?"

"I'll take the same as you if I may, sir."

Leon nodded. "Of course."

"And some ammunition," Michael said. "We don't know how many enemies we'll encounter." He took some magazines for the Glocks and the shotguns out of the bag and handed some to Leon before squirrelling some away in his own pockets.

Devon led them out of the room and to a door marked PRIVATE. She opened the door to reveal a small room with a magic circle painted in red on the floor. White candles surrounded the circle. Devon lit all of them.

The candlelight illuminated an altar that sat at one end of the room. Upon the altar was a black cloth with a white embroidered pentagram. Sitting on the cloth, a small cauldron began to emit a thick, pungent smoke, despite the fact that there was no heat source beneath it. The smoke smelled of flowers and berries that Leon didn't recognize.

"Stand in the circle," Victoria directed.

Leon and Michael stepped over the candles and stood together in the center of the magic circle.

"When you need to come back, call me," Devon said, handing Leon a card with her number on it.

She then crouched down behind the altar for a moment and stood up again with a silver bowl in one hand and two small daggers in the other. She handed the daggers to Leon and Michael and held out the bowl. Leon could see herbs and leaves in there. "I need a drop of blood from each of you," Devon said.

Leon nicked his finger and squeezed some blood out of the tiny wound and into the bowl. Michael did the same. Victoria took the daggers from them while Devon took the bowl to the altar.

Both women began chanting in languages that were unknown to Leon and that, he was sure, did not belong in the modern world.

An energy began to rise within the circle. Leon felt the hair on his arms stand on end.

The witches continued their chanting and the energy started to spin around the circle. As the sisters increased the speed of their words, so the speed of the energy became faster.

Then Devon tipped the contents of the silver bowl into the cauldron. The pungent smoke turned red and then Leon couldn't see the room anymore.

He and Michael were now standing on the deck of a forty-foot yacht floating in the Atlantic Ocean.

16

When Mallory and I got back to the house, I checked my phone. I had six missed calls and eight texts from Leon and two missed calls from Felicity. Leon's texts ranged from him asking me where I was to insinuating that I had better things to do than meet him.

I called him and got his voicemail.

"Hey, Leon, give me a call as soon as you get this."

After hanging up, I called Victoria Blackwell. I'd mentioned my plan to use a locator spell to find Lucy and I assumed he'd gone ahead with that plan."

"Alec, how nice to hear from you!" Victoria said. "How are you?"

"I'm fine," I said. "I'm looking for Leon. Is he

there with you?"

"No, dear, he isn't here."

"Oh, I thought he might have dropped by your place and asked you to cast a locator spell."

"Yes, he did that. We cast the spell and now he's gone to rescue Lucy and Brad Hawthorne."

"Okay. Can you give me the address? I'll see if he needs any help."

"There isn't an address exactly."

"No address. So can you just tell me where he is?"

"He's on a boat in the Atlantic."

"What?"

"He's on a—"

"I heard what you said. How did he get there?"

"We sent him there. And if he doesn't call us in the next five minutes, we can't get him back."

Mallory was in the kitchen filling the coffee machine. I stuck my head through the doorway and said, "I need to go and see to the Blackwell sisters. They've sent Leon onto a boat, apparently, and he may be stuck there. You want to stay here or come with?"

"I'll come with you," she said, pushing the coffee machine aside. "Let's go."

We went out to the Land Rover and I backed out past the Shadow Watch SUV, which I'd left on the street with the keys in the ignition. I was sure someone from the organization would come by and pick it up. Just so long as they didn't disturb me in the process, that was fine.

I put the wipers on to clear the rain from the Land Rover's windshield and put my foot down hard on the gas pedal. I had no idea what kind of mess the Blackwell sisters had gotten Leon into but it didn't sound good. If there was any way I could help my friend, I was going to do it.

"I didn't mention this earlier," I said to Mallory, "But Felicity has been doing some research into the death curse. She was in England for a while and she found out some useful stuff. She thinks there's a way to reverse the spell. Apparently it involves putting Tia's heart back into her body."

She'd been looking out of the window at the rain. Now she turned to me, tears in her eyes. "I knew you'd find a way."

"It was Felicity who did the research."

"I know. When I say "you," I mean you and people you surround yourself with. They're all good people. They put their lives in the line to help others."

"You're one of those people too," I said.

She smiled, wiped a tear from her cheek and stared out of the window again.

When we arrived at Blackwell Books, we took swords from the back of the Land Rover and went straight to the room at the back of the shop, the room I knew the sisters used for their transportation spell.

I opened the door and recoiled at the smell of marigolds and hawthorn berries. The room was full of thick smoke and I had to wave my hand in front of my face to be able to see.

The Blackwell sisters stood by the altar, staring at a Devon's phone.

"Has he called?" I asked.

They both looked up and shook their heads.

I stepped into the circle and beckoned Mallory to do likewise. "Get us there," I told the Blackwells.

Victoria shook her head. "We can't. Leon might call us with seconds to spare. If we're casting the spell to send you to the boat, we can't cast the spell to bring him back."

I left the circle, frustrated that I couldn't help my friend.

Devon's phone rang. She answered the call and said, "What? What does that mean? Oh, okay. We'll do it now." She turned to Victoria and said, "He's ready to come back."

"What was the confusion when you answered the phone?" Victoria asked.

Devon frowned. He said, "Four to beam up, Scotty."

"Oh," Victoria said. "How strange."

They began to chant the spell, chanting words that meant nothing to me. The air in the room suddenly felt electrified. The smoke that had been drifting lazily over the magic circle began to swirl, gaining momentum with each passing second until it formed a miniature tornado, sucking all of the smoke in the room into its spinning wall.

Victoria and Devon's chants, which had been disparate until this moment, merged into one and now I could see shapes within the smoke. The chanting ended, the spell was done, and the swirling vortex settled, revealing Leon, Michael, Lucy, and Brad.

Leon and Michael were brandishing guns. Lucy and Brad looked shaken.

"What happened?" I asked Leon.

"You're going to want to see this," Leon said.

To Victoria and Devon, he said, "Can you send us back?"

"But the window of opportunity," Devon protested.

"It's still open. We anchored the boat. It's still over the wreck."

"All right," Devon said. "But we'll need a moment to prepare the spell."

"Good," I said. "I need some fresh air." I opened the door and we all stepped out into the bookshop.

Lucy and Brad still looked shaken so I led them to a reading nook that was furnished with easy chairs and sat them both down. "How are you guys doing?"

Lucy looked at me with fear in her eyes. She was trembling. "I only wanted to talk about the Midnight Cabal. It was just a bit of fun, like solving a mystery. I didn't mean for this to happen."

"Her posts on the Emerald Tablet website attracted the attention of the wrong people," Leon said.

"I didn't realize they were reading everything I wrote in there," Lucy said.

I looked at Leon. "The Cabal?"

He nodded. "And you're going to love what

we found on their boat. In fact, we're going to need a bag to bring some of it back with us." He went into another room and came out with a canvas bag.

Victoria stuck her head out of the room. "We're ready, boys."

"And girl," I said, indicating Mallory. "You're coming too, right?"

She shook her head. "No, you go ahead. I'll stay here with Brad and Lucy. It sounds like they've been through an ordeal; they probably need someone to talk to right now."

"Okay. Michael, you coming?"

Michael had been cleaning his shotgun. He looked up and nodded. "Yes, sir, I'm right behind you."

The three of us entered the room and stepped into the circle. Devon handed out knives and we cut ourselves before dripping blood into her silver bowl of herbs.

The spell began and the smoke filled the room. It swirled around us as the witch sisters chanted and then, when Devon poured the herbs and leaves from the bowl into the cauldron, everything changed. We were suddenly standing on the deck of a boat bobbing in the ocean.

I guessed it to be a forty-foot yacht. It had a small aft deck, on which we now stood, and a large foredeck. A set of steps led up to the bridge where the boat's control consoles were housed along with its navigation systems.

There were two bodies on the deck, both dressed in black. Pools of bright blood mingled with the rainwater on the deck where they lay.

"There were six of them," Leon said. "The other four are below decks."

He led me up to the bridge and when we got inside, out of the rain, pointed at a laptop sitting on a table. "I reckon there's going to be navigational data on that computer. We can find out where this boat's been and where they were taking Lucy and Brad." He put the laptop into the canvas bag and said, "The mother lode is below decks, though."

I followed him back down the steps to the aft deck and then through a door that led to a living area.

"Down here," Leon said, opening another door that led down to sleeping quarters. "Those two are just bedrooms," he said, indicating two closed doors. "That's where we put the other bodies. What you're gonna love is what's behind door number three."

He slid the door open and I could see that this room had been turned into a study. There was a desk bolted to the floor and another laptop.

"Look in the drawers," he said as he slid the computer into the bag.

I opened the desk drawers and discovered an array of storage devices, both electronic and more old-fashioned. Thumb drives and external hard drives sat among a stack of notebooks.

There was probably information stored on these devices that revealed Cabal locations and personnel. I tossed them into the bag alongside the computers. "Great work, Leon."

He grinned.

"Now let's get the hell out of here unless there's anything else you want to show me."

"No, that's it. Isn't that enough?"

"More than enough."

We went up to the aft deck where Michael was standing with his trusty shotgun in hand, keeping watch.

"We'll weigh anchor before we call the Blackwells," Leon said. "Let the boat drift. By the time the Cabal recover it, we'll be long gone."

He went up to the bridge and I heard a mechanical clanking sound as the anchor was retracted. Leon came back down the steps and called Devon. "I won't bother with the Star Trek jokes this time," he said. After dialing the number, he simply told Devon that we were ready to return.

We waited in the rain for a few moments before a vortex of energy seemed to rise around us. I could feel my hair stand on end and I smelled marigolds and hawthorn berries.

The boat and the sea were replaced suddenly with the smoky room in Blackwell Books. I stepped out of the circle and out of the room.

Mallory was sitting in the reading nook, talking with Brad and Lucy. They each had a glass of something that looked like sherry, no doubt provided by the Blackwell sisters.

Leon and Michael came out of the room, smoke trailing after them. Leon had the bag of goodies slung over his shoulder. "This stuff is probably protected with some high-grade security," he said. "You want me to take it home and see if I can hack into it?"

"That'd be great," I said. "I'll take the notebook."

He set the bag down and pulled the notebook out of it. He handed it to me and I flicked through the pages. It seemed to be written in some sort of code. Breaking it shouldn't be too much of a problem for Felicity.

"Felicity," I said. "I forgot to call her." I fished my phone out of my pocket and dialed Felicity's number.

"Alec," she said when she answered. "I called you hours ago."

"Yeah, I was kind of tied up. You okay?"

"I'm at the police station. Where are you?"

"Blackwell Books. What are you doing at the police station?"

"It's a long story. I thought you'd be at home."

"Also a long story."

"I want to run something by you."

"Go ahead."

"I'd rather do it face to face than over the phone."

"Well I'm going home now so you can come over when you're done at the station. You don't need me to bail you out or anything do you?"

"Very funny. I'll be over in a while."

17

Felicity arrived half an hour later. Mallory had gone to bed and I was sitting on the sofa poring over the coded notebook we'd found on the yacht. No matter how many times I tried to decipher sections of it, I came up with nada. This was more Felicity's field of expertise.

I opened the door for her and she came inside smelling of rain and a hint of perfume.

"You want tea?" I asked.

She shook her head. "I had a drink at the station. How is Mallory?"

"Sleeping again."

"That's probably the best thing she can do at the moment. Give her body and mind time to rest and heal."

"Yeah. So how is the Hawthorne case going?"

"That's what I came to speak to you about."

"Have a seat and tell me about it."

She sat on the easy chair and told me about her evening, from the moment Leon had discovered the details of the car wreck to the moment Abigail Libby had shown her a photo of Owen and Mason in tuxedos.

"So they were meant to attend the party that night," I said. "Were either of them owners of local businesses?"

"No, they both worked on the family farm," she said.

"I wonder why they were invited. Do they have any connection to the Hawthorne family?"

"Not that I can see. What I find weird about that night is the fact that Charles Hawthorne was driving near the Libby farm at all. It's miles away from his house. Doesn't it seem too coincidental that he'd be miles away from the party and crash into two people who were going to that same party?"

"I guess so."

"And the place where the accident occurred

is very close to the Libby farm. What was Charles doing there?"

"Maybe he knew the Libby family."

"Okay, let's say he knew them and he wanted to speak to them for some reason. They were on their way to the party anyway so why not just wait there for them to arrive?"

"Yeah, you have a point. So if they were on their way to the party and he left the party specifically to meet them before they got there, maybe he was trying to stop them from attending."

Her eyebrows knitted together behind her glasses. "That makes sense, I suppose, but why would he do that?"

"His wife is in charge of the invitations," I said. "Maybe she invited them but he didn't want them there for some reason."

The notebook I'd used the first time I'd met Charles in the folly was on the coffee table. I opened it and reviewed my notes from that meeting. "His wife had an affair," I said. "He knew about it."

"What if she was having an affair with one of the Libbys?"

"I guess that's possible. In fact, if it was one of the brothers, I'd say it was definitely Mason."

"Why do you say that?"

"I asked Charles if the affair might still be going on today and he said he was positive that his wife and her lover don't see each other anymore. If Mason had been Jane's lover, that would explain Charles's certainty about it being over. She can't have an affair with someone who's dead."

"Perhaps he was driving out to the Libby farm to confront Mason and tell him not to come to the party."

"Or he drove the Libby car off the road on purpose," I offered. "His lawyers stepped in and did their thing and he got away with murder."

Felicity pondered that for a minute or so. "Yes, it certainly seems possible. So a year later, Owen decides to attack Charles with magic."

"But why wait a year?" I asked.

"It probably took him that long to discover that magic worked, learn the spells he needed, and put his plan into action."

"That makes sense. His attacks would culminate in the resurrection of his brother and the death of Charles so he had to track down and learn a resurrection spell. That would take time."

"But he didn't do it on his own," Felicity

said. "There's no way he could get his wheelchair into the cellar where we saw that grave. Someone else did that part."

"And that person killed Owen," I said.

"It has to be Jane Hawthorne. She must have loved Mason enough to commit murder to bring him back."

"So why didn't the crystal shard glow when we checked her at the party?"

She thought about that for a while. "Because Owen did all the magic leading up to and including the smoke attack at the party and Jane only performed the final act, the Conjuration of the Midnight Blood. Which she did the day after the party. When we checked her, she hadn't cast the spell yet."

"Yeah, that's what I was thinking too. We should probably go find Mason and put him down. We can't have a zombie wandering around in the woods."

Felicity's eyes went wide. "Oh my God, what if he isn't in the woods? Amy and I assumed he was on foot because we saw Abigail's car outside the house. But that was when we thought Abigail had cast the spell. If it was Jane who resurrected Mason, she could have driven him from the farm in her car. The security around the Hawthorne mansion isn't going to protect Charles if Jane simply drives Mason through the gate."

I grabbed my phone and tried to call Charles. There was no answer.

Felicity was already at the front door. I followed her outside and we climbed into the Land Rover.

"Keep trying to reach him on the phone," I said, handing her my phone as I started the engine.

As I sped along the street, the rain hit the windshield in rhythmic bursts, ticking off each precious second.

When we got to the gate of the Hawthorne mansion, the guard peered lazily from the booth. "What do you want? It's late."

"Charles Hawthorne is in danger," I said. "Let us in now!"

He snorted. "Yeah, right, pal. You can turn your vehicle around and get the hell out of here."

I opened my door and slid out of the Land Rover. The guard went for his gun but before he managed to free it from his belt, I had an enchanted dagger pressed against his neck. "Open the gate now," I said calmly.

"Okay, okay. The button is inside the booth."

"So let's go press it."

We went into the booth together and he pressed the button. The gate swung open.

"Have you opened the gate for Mrs Hawthorne recently?" I asked.

"Yeah, she got back a couple of minutes ago."

I ran out of the booth and jumped into the Land Rover, flooring the gas so hard that we lurched forward. I forced myself to ease up on the pedal and drove into the parking area. The Land Rover skidded to a stop on the gravel when I slammed the brakes on.

Felicity and I got out and grabbed our swords. We sprinted across the gravel to the front door. It was closed and locked. From somewhere inside, I heard Charles Hawthorne scream, No! No, please!"

There wasn't time to find another way into the house. I sliced my sword through the heavy wooden door and angled it upward toward the top hinge. The hinge broke and I did the same with the one lower down. It only took a few seconds before I was kicking the door down. It fell into the foyer with a crash loud enough to wake the dead.

We ran inside and I shouted, "Charles, where are you?"

"Up here!" came a cry from somewhere on the floor above. "Hurry!"

I raced up the stairs to a long corridor lined with many doors. Only one of them was open. I dashed through it and saw Charles cowering in his wheelchair by the window as a creature dressed in rotting clothes shambled toward him. The stench in the air was stomach churning.

The creature that had once been Mason Libby turned to look at me with one milky eye. The other eye was gone, leaving only an empty socket Surely this monstrosity wasn't what Jane Hawthorne had envisioned rising from the grave when she'd cast the Conjuration of the Midnight Blood.

Surely she hadn't committed murder just so that this abomination of rotting flesh and crumbling bones could walk again.

I swung my sword at its neck. The blade sliced through the bloodless flesh and decayed spine as if it were nothing and the head of the creature fell to the floor.

Even decapitated, the body continued its relentless march toward Charles. A second swing of my sword took its right arm off, severing it from the torso just below the shoulder.

Felicity stepped in and swung at the monster's hips. Her sword sliced through the zombie like a hot knife through butter and the torso tumbled to the floor. Still the legs walked forward.

I hacked and slashed until they were nothing more than formless pieces of meat lying motionless on the carpet.

Charles sat trembling in his chair, his panicked eyes roaming over the disconnected pieces of the zombie, probably wondering if they were going to come back to life and reform into the shape of Mason Libby.

"Where's Jane?" I asked him.

"I don't know. She set that...thing...on me and then left."

I pointed at the flesh on the floor with my sword. "Get your butler to burn that. All of it."

He nodded.

We turned to leave the room but as we did, I saw something fall past window outside and then heard a sickening thud.

I went to the window and opened it. Jane Hawthorne lay on the gravel below. I leaned out of the window and looked up. The third floor window was open. That was where she'd jumped.

"How terrible," Felicity said, gazing down at the lifeless body on the gravel below us.

"She probably thought she didn't have a choice," I said. "She knew she'd be arrested for the murder of Owen Libby and didn't want to spend the rest of her days in prison."

"Or she was so distraught at what her love had become that she decided to go with him to the afterlife."

"That's certainly a different way of looking at it."

She turned away from the window. "I'm probably just a romantic at heart."

I looked down at the crumpled body on the gravel. "So was Jane Hawthorne, probably, and look where that got her."

When Halloween arrived, I threw a party at my place. The house was festooned with cardboard monsters and fake spider webs and I set out platters of food and provided plenty of drink. It wasn't anywhere near as pompous as the Hawthorne Fall party but I liked it even better for that reason.

I'd take my down-to-earth friends over Dearmont's elite any day and the food at my party included cakes and cookies provided by Felicity. I even had deviled eggs.

The Hawthorne case was closed and I'd been paid well by Charles Hawthorne. I still had questions about what exactly happened that night when he'd driven out to the Libby place. Had the accident been just that, an accident, or had something more sinister taken place that night?

I could find out for sure by using an old spell, an alcoholic potion, and a faerie stone. The trees by the of the road would tell me what happened. I intended to ask them someday but right now, I was going to relax while I got the chance.

Once Leon hacked into the Cabal computers and Felicity decoded the notebook, I had a feeling there were going to be some big battles ahead. The Cabal wouldn't go down without one hell of a fight.

Taking a beer to the sofa, I sat and listened to the music for while. I'd left Leon in charge of the tunes and he'd put together a playlist that included The Misfits, Ramones, and David Bowie.

"Hey, how's it going? Can I join you?"

Lucy was standing in front of the sofa, beer in hand.

"Of course."

She sat next to me and said, "Are your cases always this bad?"

"Bad?"

"Yeah, I mean like tearing families apart and stuff. I know you didn't tear my family apart and that it was already coming apart at the seams but is this the kind of thing you deal with all the time?"

"Sometimes," I said. "Not always."

"Well that's good to know. And thanks for inviting me tonight. I don't usually go to parties; they aren't really my scene."

"I'd have thought a Halloween party would be totally your scene."

"Yeah, I see what you mean, me being a horror writer and all. Hey, I should tell you about my latest idea. It's a series of books about a P.I. I was hoping you'd help me with the research."

I laughed. "Maybe."

"You still owe me an interview, remember?"

"I thought that conversation we just had was the interview."

"No way, I need a lot of in-depth information from you."

I felt a heavy hand on my shoulder and looked up to see Merlin towering over me. "What do you want?" I asked him.

"Nothing in particular, Alec, I simply wanted to commend you on the party. And thank you for the invite.'

Actually, I hadn't invited him and his

appearance was a surprise to me. "It's probably not as grand as some banquets you've attended in the past," I said. "And by past, I mean way, way in the past."

"True, I have been a guest at many grand occasions and dined with kings and queens as well as knights and princesses but this homely gathering is very pleasant. You have a lot of good and loyal friends."

"Actually, that's something I wanted to talk to you about," I told him.

"Oh?" He sat down in the easy chair and leaned forward, interested.

"When we take down the Cabal," I said, "I assume you're going to leave us and return the sheriff to his body."

He nodded. "That is our agreement."

"It's going to take a little time for us to decipher the Cabal notebook and get something useful from their computer so I have a proposition for you."

"I'm listening."

"In the meantime, I want to help Mallory, one of my friends. What we need to do is going to be perilous and we're going to need all the help we can get. Would you consider being a part of the team?"

"You mean you want me to be part of the Doggy Gang?"

"That's Scooby Gang."

He nodded. "Yes, I'd like that very much."

"Great, that's settled then."

Grinning, he stood up and went over to a bunch of guests to mingle, or at least mingle as well as an ancient wizard can at a modern day Halloween party.

"So," Lucy said, "What's this perilous quest you're about to undertake?"

"It involves the heart of a sorceress, an ancient curse, and an evil Egyptian priest."

"Sounds fun."

I took a swallow of my beer and nodded. "Yeah, it's gonna be a blast."

THE END

The series continues in TWILIGHT HEART. Get your copy now!

CPSIA information can be obtained
at www.ICGtesting.com
Printed in the USA
BVHW031323180920
589140BV00001B/22